Silent Retreat

www.amplifypublishinggroup.com

SILENT RETREAT

©2025 Sally Quinn. All Rights Reserved. No part of this publication may be reproduced, stored in a retrieval system or transmitted in any form by any means electronic, mechanical, or photocopying, recording or otherwise without the permission of the author.

This book is a work of fiction. Any references to historical events, real people, or real places are used fictitiously. Other names, characters, places and events are products of the author's imagination, and any resemblance to actual events, places or persons, living or dead, is entirely coincidental.

Epigraph: From A NEW PATH TO THE WATERFALL copyright © 1989 by the Estate of Raymond Carver. Used by permission of Grove/Atlantic, Inc. Any third-party use of this material, outside of this publication, is prohibited.

For more information, please contact:
Subplot Publishing, an imprint of Amplify Publishing Group
620 Herndon Parkway, Suite 220
Herndon, VA 20170
info@amplifypublishing.com

Library of Congress Control Number: 2024926949
CPSIA Code: PRV0225A
ISBN-13: 979-8-89138-552-8

Printed in the United States

For Father Maurice Flood
of Holy Cross Abbey
Who gave me the courage to go on

Also for Quinn and Fabiola and Khloe
Who make me happy

And as always
for Ben

ALSO BY

Sally Quinn

Finding Magic: A Spiritual Memoir

Happy Endings: A Novel

The Party: A Guide to Adventurous Entertaining

Regrets Only: A Novel

We're Going to Make You a Star

Silent Retreat

a novel

Sally Quinn

SUBPLOT
an imprint of Amplify Publishing Group

Late Fragments
by Raymond Carver

And did you get what
you wanted from this life, even so?
I did.
And what did you want?
To call myself beloved,
to feel myself
beloved on the earth.

Monday

I recognized him the minute he got out of the car. He was taller than I'd expected. Tall and lanky with an easy, confident grace about him. His salt and pepper hair was thick and curled around the back of his neck. He wore dark glasses so I couldn't see his eyes, but he cocked his head a bit to look around the property and I saw that firm jaw and half expectant smile on his lips. He was wearing jeans, a blue shirt, a light brown leather jacket, and loafers. Before the driver was able to hand over his hanging bag and satchel, he'd reached into the trunk, retrieved his luggage and a guitar case, and started toward the entrance of the retreat house.

Standing in the dining room, I tried to recall the names of the guests which were posted on the bulletin board in the entrance reception room along with their room numbers. I hadn't seen his name. But then I wouldn't have recognized it. On the sheet of paper with the names, mine read S. Sumner. Now I remembered. There was a

J. Kelly. That's all it had said. It did not say James Fitzmaurice-Kelly, Archbishop of Dublin.

I had noticed that J. Kelly had the room directly opposite mine. It was right next to the entrance of the lovely little private chapel which was attached to the retreat house. He was B7. I was B8. His room faced southeast overlooking the cow pastures and the Shenandoah mountains. My room faced southwest, overlooking the hills but also the road up to the main historic house and dormitories where the monks lived and the church services were held.

I filled my mug with tea, then waited, eyeing the U-shaped wooden table that was already set for dinner. I didn't want to just run into him in the entryway. He wouldn't know me and I would feel I had to introduce myself but I was already in silence and couldn't talk. I slipped into the kitchen as he came through the front door. I could hear him as he walked to the bulletin board to find his name and room number on the list. There were also many instructions on the board, times of services throughout the day and night, times of meals, and a sign-up sheet for private counseling with one of the monks in residence. I heard the archbishop shift around as he was reading. I didn't think he would recognize my name. As it turned out there were only about three or four other people attending. It would be a quiet week.

I waited until the same monk that had greeted me had welcomed His Grace into the front hall. The monk was sweet looking, much older, and balding, wearing a white habit and flip flops. Flush-faced and rotund, he was Friar Tuck in *Robin Hood*. Perfect. I hadn't wanted the monk to carry my luggage either, and I watched as Fitz gently wrestled his leather handbag onto his own shoulder before going out to the hallway and down the stairs to the floor below.

I gave him about ten minutes before I followed him and approached my room. The doors were always unlocked. No keys. I quickly opened mine and collapsed on the bed. I was hot and tired from my afternoon walk, but more than that I was made deeply uncomfortable by his presence. I had come here to spend five days alone, to get away from my marriage, to try to make sense of my life, to pull myself together, to have privacy. And now he was here, and I didn't know how to feel.

Spraig had made fun of me when I told him I was going to a Trappist monastery for a silent retreat for five days.

"Jesus, Sybilla," he had said. "I can't believe you're going in for all of that mumbo jumbo."

This wasn't the first time my husband had been contemptuous of me or made me feel diminished. Why couldn't he, just once, have said, "Oh, really? What compels you to do that? What do you hope to get out of it? Where did you get the idea?" He really wasn't capable of thinking that way or even using those words. Introspection was not one of his many attributes. I knew that. I understood who he was. Why did I keep hoping for some miraculous change in him where he would suddenly become interested in what I was doing, what I thought, what I had accomplished?

He was very famous: a brilliant New York television interviewer. He had his own nightly show at eleven. He was asked to moderate every conference worth anything around the globe with world leaders and celebrities. His show was the place to be seen whether launching a book, a movie, or a campaign. He couldn't walk down the street without people stopping him, telling him how much they admired him, asking him for autographs or, more recently, selfies. Dinner in restaurants was a nightmare. People coming up to the table constantly just to shake his hand, wanting to chat. There was no way one could actually enjoy a meal. I found myself often drinking too much wine just to get through the evening. It wasn't as if he asked the maître d' to seat them in the back of the room with him facing the wall and quietly suggesting to well-wishers that they did not want to be disturbed as some celebrities did. Oh no, he had to have the table in the front of the room so everyone would see him. If he wasn't approached, he would get up and work the room himself, glad-handing his admirers, leaving me alone, even abandoning our dinner partners. He almost always failed to introduce me. I had recently begun to hold out my hand and introduce myself, "Hi, I'm Sybilla Sumner," just to make the point that I was not invisible. I occasionally thought of adding, "of *The New Yorker*," but could never really bring myself to do it.

We were heading toward our fifteenth wedding anniversary. I had no enthusiasm for celebrating. He, of course, wanted a big bash in the Hamptons. The last thing I would ever consider.

What, one might ask, did I ever see in him? Well, for one thing he was dazzling. In every way. Once I got over his good looks—tall, athletic, blue-eyed, blond, and his radiant smile which seemed only for me—I was captivated by his slow, sensuous southern drawl. A Savannah boy, he was an exotic. I'd never been out with anybody but Yankees. He really did eat grits, okra, black-eyed peas, and country ham. He drank sweet tea and bourbon. He said y'all. He might as well have been covered with hanging moss. He didn't have a bad CV either. BMOC at Princeton, President of the Ivy Club, Captain of the

Debate Team, Captain of the Fencing Team, Captain of the Tennis Team, magna cum laude in politics. He was a man with ambition, a man on the move, an exciting man to be with. He was outgoing and fun, sexy, and clever. And he thought I hung the moon.

THE DINNER BELL WAS RINGING. I didn't know why I was so nervous at the thought of being in the same room with the archbishop. I think it was the fact that my knowing who he was and him not knowing who I was made me wobbly. Just seeing him on TV I had been so struck by him, far more than any man I had ever met. He was extraordinary: brilliant, empathetic, thoughtful, open-minded, courageous. There was a soulfulness about him I couldn't quite describe, although I sensed that he was in some kind of pain. Never mind that he was good-looking and sexy.

I stood and paced my room. It was as I had expected. Monastic. But comfortable and cozy. Green wall-to-wall carpeting, a single bed with a blue quilted spread and one pillow, a beige wooden armchair, a bedside table with a lamp, cream cotton curtains, and a wooden built-in desk with a lamp. Above the desk hung a crucifix and on the desk was a Holy Bible. The utilitarian bathroom was all white with a shower and four tiny rounds of soap. Oddly, it felt just right. It was a room without a story. The story would be mine to make. I didn't bother to shower or change. The September days, although hot, were dry, and the nights were cooler. Besides, I had one more service after supper. I, too, was wearing jeans and a blue shirt. I ran a brush through my hair. Did I detect a gray hair in the midst of my light brown, shoulder-length locks? Did I notice a tiny wrinkle between my brows? I took one last cursory glance at my image in the small mirror and went out the door. Thankfully he wasn't coming out of his.

I had never been to a silent retreat before. It was not in my realm of social experiences. I didn't know how one could just ignore people for an entire week, at the same time eating three meals a day with them, praying or meditating together in the chapel, running into each other on walks. It was such an intimate experience, and at the same time so distant. The idea that I wouldn't be able to speak to Fitz exacerbated my uneasiness.

As I went up the stairs and into the carpeted and cozily furnished reception area, I nodded to Friar Tuck. We weren't supposed to use our cell phones and I had left Friar Tuck's number in case of emergency even though I realized it would be very difficult to fully unplug. From outside the dining room I could hear the speaker playing Gregorian chants. I smiled to myself as I imagined Spraig's eyes rolling. This was definitely going to be the full experience.

Several people were already seated at the U-shaped table. The woman who ran the kitchen came out, gave us our last verbal instructions (a short lecture on meal times and dishwashing, along with instructions to leave our name cards at the table and always sit in the same spot). She then led us in saying grace and disappeared into the back office. I'd been expecting the archbishop, but he hadn't arrived yet.

I served my plate from a small side table—corn and ham soup, cold cuts, salad, and a choice of white bread or multigrain. I filled my water glass and chose a seat as far from the other four people as I could at the end of the table closest to the door and put my name card down. Nobody looked at me, nodded or smiled. People were eating, it seemed, with grim determination, almost willing themselves not to look up or interact in any way. I took the cue. It was strange. It reminded me of eating on a plane or train except in that case nobody was on the same "journey."

I use that word lightly. It's become such a cliché. But here at the monastery we had all come looking for truth, clarity, spiritual sustenance. Everyone looked perfectly nice, casually dressed in T-shirts and pants. As I glanced around the room I saw a moon-faced man in his early sixties, balding and a little out of shape, his drooping shoulders seemed to show signs of defeat. There was a woman in her fifties, dyed blonde hair pulled back by a black velvet headband. She was very thin, to the point of looking anorexic. She was heavily made-up and wore expensive jewelry. I imagined her a renegade from Palm Beach, her falling face a testament to her dedication to alcohol. There was a handsome young Indian man in his early thirties with dark curly hair, thick eyebrows, and a clean stubble on his face. He was deep in thought, almost trance-like. He may well have been meditating. And across from him sat an angry looking woman, probably in her late forties. She was letting her frizzy black hair go gray. She seemed defiantly uninterested in her looks. She wore no makeup, was a little overweight, and had on a beige formless tunic. I concluded, despite myself, that she likely didn't shave her legs or under her arms, had been raised by hippy parents, and was unlucky in love.

They all were obviously alone. But to be alone was the point of coming to Holy Cross Abbey after all. They were clearly all in pain, as was I. I realized I was scared. I was there to examine my deepest thoughts and emotions, something I had never dared do. I was there to confront my demons, something that terrified and repulsed me. I was there to discover who I really was and determine what I really wanted, something that was completely alien to me. At the moment, it seemed easier to speculate about these strangers' lives than to begin to address my own. I wondered, as I glanced around the room again, if they were stereotyping me in my fitted jeans and blue shirt in the same way as I was them.

Fitz was exhausted. This last book tour had been grueling. It wasn't just the long hours of endless interviews, the traveling, the "being on" all the time, the lack of privacy. It was the subject matter. He knew when he wrote the book that it would be controversial. He was prepared for that. What he wasn't prepared for was the avalanche of criticism that had fallen on him.

Looking back, he probably should have seen it coming. Maybe he had been naïve. Yet the subject matter was one which had been broached for years. *Why Celibacy?* had become an overnight sensation, as they like to say in publishing. Obviously, part of the reason there had been so much outrage was because he was, in fact, the Archbishop of Dublin. He also happened to become, at forty-nine, the youngest Archbishop of Dublin in history. And though he was not at all vain, he was thought to be extremely good-looking. It embarrassed him, especially when the media referred to him as "Fabulous Fitz."

What was even more embarrassing was that now, at fifty-three, he was a celebrity, and women were always coming on to him. There was clearly nothing more enticing than the notion of bedding a celibate priest. Yet the mere title of his book only sought to increase his desirability. The truth was that he had no intention or desire to break his own vows. But he did believe that the vows were absurd, unrealistic, indefensible, against the teachings of the early Church and certainly would have been an anathema to Christ.

As he wrote in his book, the history of celibacy in the Church had only begun in the sixteenth century when the Church didn't want men marrying and leaving their lands to their spouses rather than to the Church. It was all about the money. Not only was it hypocritical, he felt, it was unchristian. He was also deeply concerned that the celibacy vows were keeping a huge number of good men from the priesthood and the Church was slowly dying.

While declaring his own choice of remaining celibate, he wrote that he believed no priest should be bound by such an inhumane vow. He also argued that it was unfair that married men from other denominations could become priests as long as they converted to Catholicism.

He had already been the recipient of the ire of the Vatican for two previous books. The first, a condemnation of the Church for its role in the child sexual abuse scandal, *Un Christian*. Although nobody could publicly denounce him—after all, who could support child sexual abuse?—it was felt he should have simply stayed silent like the rest of his colleagues rather than attack Mother Church. His last book, *Questions for the Church*, asking about homosexuality and women's roles in the Church, was met with hostile silence from everyone but the pope.

People knew better than to criticize Fitz openly. He was extremely popular in Ireland and internationally and he was seen as the pope's fair-haired boy.

Now, however, the worst had happened. With his new book out and gaining so much notoriety, he had been sent an eighteen-page letter, listing his affronts to the Church and announcing that he was being investigated. He had been summoned to Rome. His Holiness wanted to see him. This was not a good sign. Fitz even feared that he might be relieved of his position.

He had been in New York when he received the letter. He had just finished on Spraig Exley's show. Spraig had always been very generous about Fitz's writing. Fitz had been on his show many times. He didn't dislike Spraig. How could he when Spraig was so complimentary to him? But he didn't much like him either. Spraig was "perfect." A Golden Boy with a too strong handshake and a studied aura of bonhomie. Fitz suspected that underneath the sheen there was a lot of insecurity. As good as he was as an interviewer, he didn't really seem to care about the people he was questioning. There was no empathy. It was all about him. He dropped names, he could be unctuous, almost fawning to the celebrities and yet Fitz had been appalled at the way he treated his staff.

As far as Fitz was concerned, his only redeeming quality was his wife, Sybilla Sumner, a reporter for *The New Yorker* who wrote the most insightful and profound pieces he had read in a long time. Though he had never met her, he had been following her writing for years and was particularly enchanted by a piece she had recently done on the Christology of the unicorn. It was an astoundingly original take on a subject that had always interested him, and something about it read differently from her other writing. It was no surprise that she had just been named a MacArthur Genius.

After coming home from the studio he'd read the letter from the Vatican closely, understanding that this would be a big turning point in his life, not only in terms of his commitment to the Church, but his devotion to God. It was then that he decided to go on retreat. He had heard about Holy Cross Abbey, a monastery in Virginia, the perfect antidote to a week in New York flogging his latest opus.

FITZ WAS LATE FOR DINNER. He had heard the bell ringing, but he'd needed to unpack and stretch his legs. Now, he splashed cold water on his face and took the stairs two at a time. People were already seated and eating almost furtively as if they were doing something wrong. He heard the Gregorian chants and smiled to himself. Well, they were certainly setting the mood. He grabbed a plate and looked around for a place to sit. There were four other people at the table. And then her. Sybilla. Passing by her, he saw her nametag and froze. *Holy mother of Christ*, he thought. *It's her!*

Everyone glanced up at him. So did she. They gazed at each other for a long moment, a spark of recognition on each of their faces. The others went back to their meals. She didn't lower her eyes. He slowly walked to one end of the table, as far away from her as possible. They continued to stare at each other. He took a seat. He caught his breath. She seemed to be a bit shaken. Finally, they both looked down. If anyone had actually seen them, they would have thought they were praying. They wouldn't be wrong.

IT WAS SUPPOSED to be a silent retreat. But at one point, poor Dave sneezed so loudly that we all nearly jumped out of our seats. We had to stop ourselves from saying "bless you" because we were not allowed to speak. Dave made mouthing motions as if to apologize. I refrained from glancing at Fitz. For some reason, I felt sure I'd find him laughing.

Dinner was over in about thirty minutes. We all scraped our chairs back on the floor at the same time, seemingly desperate to get out of there. No candlelit, wine filled, gourmet bacchanal, this. We only had about half an hour before the seven-thirty Office of Compline—the last prayer of the day, the beginning of the Great Silence, at the Monastery Chapel up the hill toward the main house.

I grabbed an orange from the fruit bowl to take to my room where I read through some of the spiritual brochures I had picked up on the hall table. I had also done a little research ahead of time and brought along some of my own.

The ones from Father Richard Rohr, a Franciscan Friar, based in Albuquerque, New Mexico, were particularly thoughtful and interesting. His writings on spirituality had always intrigued me, particularly his book *The Enneagram: A Christian Perspective* and his brilliant *Falling Upward* about the two halves of life. I was definitely headed toward the second half which is obviously why the book appealed to me so. He had also won the Thomas Merton Award, another coincidence because one of the monks at the retreat had been a friend of the famous mystic Father Merton who resided at the Abbey of Gethsemani in Kentucky. I had been a follower of Merton's since he wrote the magnificent *Seven Story Mountain*.

It was beginning to be twilight. I checked the time, ran a brush through my hair again and hurried out to the reception room. Nobody was about. They must have already left. I dashed out of the retreat house, not wanting to burst in late on the service and walked quickly up the hill, turning right to the yellow stone main house, following the sounds of the bells. I headed toward the chapel which was to the left attached to a wing connecting the house to the monks' quarters.

As I stood in the enclosure at the door to the small chapel, I could hear nothing but the ringing of the gongs. Ten times. I felt ill at ease, which I had not during the midday service. But it was sunny then and as I was the first guest to arrive, I was there alone.

Now, I breathed in and quietly opened the door. There he was. He was seated in the second row on the same bench as I was, as far to the left as possible. I couldn't help but notice that Deedee, of the blonde hair and stretched face, was sitting in the same row across the aisle. Both of their heads were bowed. I had to collect myself. I was here to surrender to the quiet. Yet my heart seemed to be making an excruciating loud thumping noise.

I took a seat on the wooden bench in the last row on the aisle. Shortly after, Krish, Dave, and Arianthe arrived. Dave and Arianthe bowed to the altar and took their seats. Krish kneeled in the aisle before sitting.

There were beams on the ceiling, modest windows, and a simple altar. On either side of the altar, away from us, were several rows of benches facing each other. The light was dim. The overhead lanterns had been turned off for Compline and the only lighting was the overhead spots among the beams, also dimmed. There were candles burning to the side of the far altar by a painting of the Virgin Mary and Jesus and a small wooden cross. I had never understood the expression "the silence was deafening" until that moment. It was as if the world had stopped. I felt guilty even inhaling. The silence was why we were there. The chapel had a totally different feeling for the two services I had attended earlier.

I heard a slight shuffling noise and saw, coming in slowly, the monks, ten of them, one by one, in white tunics with black scapulars over them, except for the novices who were all in white. They were slightly stooped over. I was shocked to see how old they were. They had white hair or were balding, some with beards, some hardly able to walk, one in a wheelchair. They bowed to the cross and took their seats along the side benches facing the altar, lowered their heads and began to pray. When they stood, and we stood with them, they began chanting their prayers.

"Glory be to the Father and to the Son and to the Holy Spirit, as it was in the beginning and now and ever shall be, world without end."

I noticed Fitz crossing himself. The abbot read from the scriptures. Psalms. We sat. We stood. We sat. We stood. They said The Lord's prayer. I could hear Fitz's clear, sure, voice. I said it too. Amen. Fitz's voice was familiar. The monks chanted again, some in quavering voices. They turned out the lights completely. Now all we could see were the flickering candles and the pale silhouettes of each other and the monks. It was hypnotic and I found myself loosening up, almost going into a trance, almost forgetting that Fitz was sitting a few rows in front of me. There was a mysterious aura about it. The darkness, the candlelight, the softly playing music. There was a solemnity about it. A finality. This was the end of the day. I felt all of my breath expel. My body relaxed. An almost unrecognizable sense of peace flowed through me. I once had a very religious friend who used to tell me, when she was having terrible problems, "I'm going to give them to God." Right at that moment I understood the compulsion. Whether or not I believed in God was irrelevant. I was overcome with relief. I could just, for this moment, turn over all of my problems to God. Not that I knew what that meant. All I can say is that I was unburdened for the first time that I could remember.

I wasn't immediately aware when it was over. I sat, my head bowed, waiting for the others to file past me before I got up to leave. I don't know how long I was there, but it was very pleasant and consoling. When I looked up, the chapel was empty. I walked back in the gloaming. I was so distracted that I almost missed the left turn to the retreat house.

Once in my room I dragged myself to the shower, brushed my teeth, set the alarm for three a.m. and fell on the bed, emotionally spent. I couldn't believe I was actually going to get up for the three-thirty a.m. Vigils, the first service of the day when the monks woke up and began their work. But I had decided to go all-in, at least for one night, to get the full experience. I don't even remember falling asleep.

Tuesday

THE ALARM ON MY PHONE for the three-thirty a.m. service went off way too soon. I staggered out of the bed, unsure of where I was. I had been having a recurring dream. I went home to find my parents' house on Beacon Hill, which was filled with antiques, cherished objects collected from around the world, mementos and family photographs, moved to an unattractive location and renovated to look like an antiseptic suburban ranch house. This dream was always so unsettling that it took me several minutes to shake it off. I washed my face, brushed my teeth, threw on my jeans from the night before, grabbed a jacket, and headed out the door.

As I passed through the entrance hall I was relieved to see a group of brightly colored flashlights standing upright on the table by the door. They looked like mini Onward Christian soldiers, marching as to war. It had been a little difficult to see coming back after Compline and I was afraid of getting lost. I took one and plunged into the darkness and the sudden chill of the autumn night. I trudged up the hill and beamed my way to the chapel. As I entered, the lights were low but not turned off. It was empty. I decided to sit in the middle of the second row to the right of the aisle this time. About ten minutes passed. It was three o'clock. Still nobody. Did I get this wrong? I was sure the schedule had a three-thirty service. How could I forget that?

Then I heard the door creak open and footsteps coming halfway down the aisle. The footsteps turned left, and I could hear them settle in the middle of the row. I didn't dare look around. Was it him? It had to be. They were a man's footsteps and they were determined, confident. No one else showed up. We were alone. The monks appeared. Did they really do this at three-thirty every morning of their lives? I would rather live in silence for the rest of my life than get up at that hour each day. Well . . . maybe not, but still.

The service was more or less the same as the one last night. This time I didn't go into a trance. All I could think of was how I was going to get out of there without running into him. It would be too awkward. We wouldn't be able to speak.

It was over way too soon. I waited for him to leave but there was no movement. I waited a bit more. Nothing. *Okay*, I thought. *I'll make a run for it.* I got up, fumbled with my jacket, walked to the aisle, and glanced up quickly to see my way. He was sitting there, head bowed. I made it to the door and out. It was only then that I realized I had left my flashlight on the bench. What was I going to do? It was dark and cold and I knew I would not be able to see my way to the retreat house. But I couldn't go back inside. It would be too embarrassing. I would just have to try to make it on my own. I couldn't even see the stairs down from the chapel. Gingerly, I started walking. I could hear the leaves crunching beneath my shoes. And past that it was pitch black. I was terrified I would end up in the bushes, or worse, flat on my face on the concrete drive just in time for him to find me with my nose smashed and bloody. But I couldn't just wait for him to come and show me the way. I couldn't speak so I couldn't tell him I had left my flashlight behind. And I certainly couldn't reach out and grab on to him as he passed me by. The damsel in distress was not my best number. I stood there paralyzed with indecision. If I tried to make it alone it would take me an hour to get back. If I even made it.

Suddenly I saw a flash and I heard someone pacing quickly toward me. Before I knew it, he was at my side, shining his light in front of me so I could find the path. I looked up at him with gratitude. He smiled at me and nodded. Together, in step with each other, we walked back to the house. At one point I tripped and he took my elbow and steadied me, then let go. I nodded at him. He smiled again. I say steadied. I was anything but steady.

Once we were back at the house, he put the flashlight on the table under the lamp. I raised my hand in a goodbye gesture and went into the hall toward the stairs. He followed me. We both walked down at the same time. He paused to let me by and I paused, too. We were so close to each other that we were nearly touching. I could feel the warmth of his body and I almost feigned tripping again so he would grab me. I knew his room was across the hall from mine. He didn't. I scurried to the end of the hall but he, with his long strides, was at his door at the same time as I was. He was clearly flustered when he realized where my room was. I saw him glance at my face for a moment, and then back down at his shoes. But he pulled himself together and as he opened his door, he turned and made a gallant bow and disappeared into his room. I opened my own door, closed it and fell back against it. *Oh God*, I implored. How could I do this for five days?

Before this last year, I'd never thought about divorcing Spraig. Divorce was a word that had always been anathema to me. For one thing, I was raised a Catholic. My mother, Segolene de Serigny, "Maman," was a devout French Catholic who attended Mass every Sunday. My father, Charles Sumner, "Father" to me, "Chip" to his buddies, the ultimate Boston WASP, was definitely one of the Frozen Chosen. They went to separate Churches on Sunday. He, to Trinity Episcopal Church in the Back Bay where we lived on Beacon Street. She, to the Cathedral of the Holy Cross. They would meet for lunch at the Somerset Club on Beacon Street—all leather chairs and "Turkey" rugs, damask curtains and chinoiserie. There he would have a martini, or "Yellow Boy," made with yellow vermouth, and always Cod Point Shirley, a seafood casserole that Maman detested. Way too Boston. For her it was a glass of Spanish sherry and Crabmeat Bordelaise. And for dessert, their one big splurge, A Soufflé Grand Marnier. I would be taken to the Catholic Church for Sunday school by my governess (my father had agreed I would be a Catholic, however we never discussed it). Afterward I would go home for lunch while my parents went to the club. That was fine with me. I thought the club was hopelessly stuffy and boring. The food was too rich, everything was made with butter and heavy cream, and they had almost no desserts. The only one I liked was the Coupe Favorite, Somerset Style which was basically strawberries, sugar, heavy cream and vanilla ice cream. Besides, my parents always got a little tipsy which I found embarrassing. Father would inevitably have a second Yellow Boy and Maman couldn't bear to see him drinking alone. We went there with the whole family for my first communion when I was seven, but then mercifully I was spared from going again until my confirmation at age thirteen when I started going to Mass with Maman and my parents insisted that I join them every Sunday for lunch. If I hadn't been an only child it wouldn't have been so tedious, but I had nobody to rebel with.

My parents had a very good marriage, despite their cultural differences. For one thing, they were both extremely attractive. Maman was a petite French beauty, tiny waisted and big bosomed, full lipped and wide-eyed, her short, fair, highlighted hair was brushed back behind her ears, slightly tousled as though she had just gotten out of bed. She had a sweet, melodic voice and her French accent was positively dripping with old world insouciance. Most men found her very sexy, but none more so than my father who could barely keep his hands off of her.

He was a jock and built like one. Broad chested, muscular, square jawed, deep voiced, slightly balding with graying sideburns and curls at the back of his neck. He had been an All-American football player at Harvard and was still remembered by the old timers as one of the greats. He was a man's man. My mother adored him. There was no question in my mind that they were still having an active sex life, which pleased and embarrassed me at the same time. It also made me jealous. They were probably getting it on a lot more than I was these days.

They had met when Father had taken a year at the Sorbonne in Paris after he graduated. He had postponed his entrance into Harvard Law School for a year and the inevitability of following in his family's footsteps as a public servant. Maman was also studying at the

Sorbonne, but in a rather desultory way. They were seated at tables next to each other having a coffee at the brasserie Les Deux Magots overlooking the church yard on le Boulevard Saint Germain. When the waiter brought Maman *l'addition* she was mortified to realize that she had forgotten her wallet. My father gallantly reached over to her table, grabbed the bill, and held it over her head, offering, in French, to pay for her as long as she would agree to join him for another cup. Stunned, she burst out laughing and replied in English that he was so brash she couldn't possibly say *non*. It was, as they say, a *coup de foudre*. They were inseparable from that moment on, and she followed him back to Boston. They were married in my family's private chapel on the Greek island of Spetses after my father's first year at law school and as far as I could see, blissfully so. In fact, now in their seventies, they had been so happy together that I often felt a little left out. Not that they didn't love me. They did. I was cherished and adored. It's just that they were often in their own world together, so devoted to each other that nobody, even I, could penetrate their bubble.

So, divorce was never in my vocabulary. In a real marriage it was unimaginable. As a Catholic (even though I would have to describe myself as lapsed) it was unthinkable. As a person of honor, it was untenable. No. Divorce was out of the question. I had made my vows to Spraig. I would keep my word. At least I always had.

Breakfast was available all morning. The kitchen was stocked with coffee, tea, different cereals, yogurt, fruit, juice, toast, hard boiled eggs and the special creamed honey and apple butter that the Monks made and sold on the property. The first (or rather the second) service of the day, Lauds, was at seven a.m. Fitz didn't want to miss the Eucharist, which was only given then.

The Eucharist was for him still the center of Catholic life. He leapt out of bed, used to getting up early for services. However, what really motivated him to get up was the thought of seeing Sybilla again. Her secret, slightly awkward, shy, knowing smile. Her arresting eyes. She had totally captivated him the moment he saw her. She was gorgeous, but in a natural, fresh, unselfconscious way. She seemed completely unaware of her own beauty.

He needed his daily run before breakfast. He slipped into his sweats and T-shirt, laced up his sneakers and hurried to Lauds. She wasn't there. He wasn't surprised. A three-thirty service and another at seven. He wasn't even sure he would make Vigils again. This week was supposed to be restful, not a penance.

After the service he ran down the main road to the front gate and back. Not a long run but enough for now. He took a quick shower. He was sorry to see there was no tub. There was nothing he loved more than a good long soak at the end of the day, nursing a glass of Irish whiskey as he pondered what was next.

He was anxious to get to breakfast, but she wasn't there. The others were slowly trickling in. He took hard boiled eggs, a piece of toast slathered with apple butter, and a glass of orange juice to his seat. They had all taken their original places. That was to be the case for the rest of their stay. He dawdled over his meal, then got a cup of coffee. No sign of her. He had another cup of coffee. He checked the time. Almost nine-thirty. He was disappointed. Was he really going to have to wait until lunch to see her? Had she left?

Fitz had wanted to be a priest as long as he could remember. The Church had been his escape, his solace. His home life had been tumultuous and destructive. His Da, Jamie Kelly, had been a jolly man with a ruddy complexion, a thick head of dark hair, a muscular physique, with an exuberant personality, who was known throughout County Wicklow as a legendary storyteller. He was always the most popular guy in the pub. Fitz's Ma, Flora McDougald, was a Scottish girl from the Isle of Jura. Her parents had run a bed and breakfast on the island but his ma wanted more of life. Her dream was to go to the world class Norland College in Bath to become a nanny. Norland nannies were known as the nannies for royalty. Her parents saved for years to send her, and she had been accepted. After graduation, she had gotten a job with a very posh family who had an estate outside of Dublin near Glendalough. It was at a pub on her day off with some of the other staff that she had met Jamie Kelly. She was immediately bowled over by his looks and his charisma. He in turn, was smitten with this bright-eyed, smiling, arrestingly lovely young redheaded Scottish lass. Within months, much to her parents' shock, Norland College's embarrassment, and her employer's outrage, she quit her job and eloped with Jamie. It was the biggest mistake she ever made. Jamie had been a promising young insurance salesman when they met but, rather quickly, when his job seemed not to go well, he took to drinking and spending more time at the pub than with Flora. At first it seemed manageable. Fitz was born and was the joy of her life. They named him after his Da who was a distant relative of the esteemed writer of the same name. After Fitz was born, Jamie began losing his jobs because of the drink. The more he drank, the more he failed. The drink and the subsequent loss of jobs took its toll, and he lived in a darkening circle of shame and guilt and grief. When he drank, he was no longer the cheery soul beloved by all but a bitter creature of self-loathing. Of course, he took it out on Fitz and his ma. Fitz was only about four when he began to realize that Da had a serious problem. He and his mum both tried to protect each other from his rages but his mum had her own problems. After Fitz was born, she had had several miscarriages and one stillborn and had never been able to conceive again. Flora McDougald had been dragged down to the depths of despair, not just because of the losses but because of her husband's reaction to them. Fitz understood early on that it was up to him to keep his mum together. He held her and stroked her hair when she would take to her bed sobbing. He told her he loved her. She would hold him too and they would cradle each other. She called him *astoirin*—my little treasure. But he couldn't seem to make her better. He had adored his da but he began to loathe him for his seeming lack of compassion for his mum as well as loathing himself for his inability to console her. Flora's downward spiral into depression soon became a clinical problem and she was diagnosed as being bipolar. Her trips and long stays in the hospital over the years became more and more frequent as did his da's absences in the evenings. Fitz was left to fend for himself, foraging for leftovers in the kitchen and depending on what his da would bring home from the pub. Yet he never doubted that both of his parents loved him in their own ways. He was, after all, their only child.

Glendalough (Glen of Two Lakes) was a glacial valley outside of

Dublin, one of the most beautiful sites in all of Ireland. St. Kevin had founded the early medieval monastic settlement in the sixth century. Glendalough was a magical place and its soul-satisfying beauty was one of the reasons that Fitz was able to survive. When Jamie wasn't three sheets to the wind, he would pack a picnic and take Fitz up to the lakes where the views were breathtaking, and they'd have a father-son outing together. Fitz exalted in those days. Jamie was a hugger. He hugged everybody including Fitz. But those trips were few and far between. His mum was a baker and when she was well, she would have Scottish tea cakes ready for him when he got home from school. He would run down to the bottom of the hill from school, which was right near the church, to their little white stone cottage with the green shutters and door. When there was smoke curling up from the chimney that was a good sign. It meant his mum was there. He would throw himself in her arms, she would fluff his hair, fuss over him, kiss him and hold his hands. They would sit by the fire together, all cozy, where she did her needlepoint and would tell him tales of her family's illustrious history and Scottish lore. The Celtic myths were his favorites, especially those about the unicorn.

The unicorn was Scotland's national animal, the female a symbol of purity and innocence, the male a symbol of masculinity and power. *Aon-Adharcach* is what she called it. His mum had a large needlepoint wall hanging she had made herself of the Scottish Coat of Arms, the unicorn on the left. *Dieu et Mon Droit* was stitched into the bottom and around the shield was *Honi Soit Qui Mal Y Pense*. "Evil to one who thinks it." His mum liked to call herself a unicorn aficionado. Their little cottage was chock full of unicorns of all sizes and shapes. They had unicorn salt and pepper shakers, unicorn figurines, unicorn lamps, unicorn everything. Many of the pillows and rugs she had made had unicorns on them. It drove his da around the bend. "Bloody unicorns," he would grumble with feigned annoyance as he propped himself up in his chair with his unicorn pillow, picked up his whiskey glass etched with unicorns, and listened to her stories. Those were the good days, when they were getting along.

Gradually those times stopped. She would go off to the hospital for a few weeks and when she was home she was distant, clearly drugged and spent most of her time in bed. At this point, Fitz, as an eight-year-old, was completely taking care of himself. Both of his parents had once been devout Catholics but after the losses of the babies their church-going stopped.

If it hadn't been for his uncle, Diarmid, his father's brother, Fitz may have ended up in an orphanage. Diarmid Kelly was the parish priest at St. Kevin's, the local church in Glendalough where they had grown up. Fitz had begun going to Sunday school at an early age. But it wasn't the school he loved as much as the Mass. He loved everything about the ritual. He loved the bells and the incense and the hypnotic chanting and the Latin and the vestments. It was calming and reassuring. Mass was literally his sanctuary, the only place where he could find peace in his life. What made the church so appealing was its simplicity. There were high rafters, a stone altar overlaid with driftwood, plain blue cushions, an antique organ, an icon of Our Lady in the entrance, and of course candles burning day and night. He always lit two candles for his parents and another for his dead siblings. Sometimes it would take all of his pocket money to put coins in the box. The one thing he didn't like was confession. He had only one sin to confess, over and over again. He had been unable to help his parents. For that he felt shame and guilt and fear. Those feelings would stay with him for much of his life.

Fitz particularly loved the Eucharist. Uncle Diarmid and most Catholics believed in transubstantiation, where the bread and wine actually turned into the body and blood of Christ. Fitz never bought it. For him, the Eucharist was a pathway to God and an affirmation of joining Christ's mission in the world.

He liked to linger after Mass to pray alone and catch the light from the stained-glass windows. If the sun was shining through, he would tell himself that God loved him. If it wasn't, he'd be in trouble. Often, he would stay and have lunch with his uncle. Afterward he would walk in the soft air past the raised graveyard and its beautiful Garden of the Virgin with views of the verdant hills in the background. He could hear the reassuring sound of the sheep bleating on the hill and he would take his time getting to the house for fear of what he would find or not find.

Diarmid knew the situation at home. He tried to help out, to bring food, to slip money to Flora for heating and sundries. But more and more she wasn't there and Jamie would be at the pub or passed out on the sofa and Fitz would be alone. He always put on a brave face for his uncle, but his defense of his parents became increasingly unconvincing. It was apparent after a while that Fitz could not be allowed to stay there unattended, so Diarmid had him move in with him to the parish house. The parish house became his home. Not just physically but spiritually as well. It often felt that God had forgiven him his sins and brought him home, and there he would stay. As he'd grown older, he had always seen his writing as an extension of his beliefs. Even the celibacy book had called him toward the Church rather than away from it. He had never wavered in his faith since. But in recent years, that had been changing.

The letter from the Vatican only reinforced that. For the first time since he had entered seminary, he felt untethered.

I DIDN'T EVEN WAKE UP again until after nine. I was completely wiped out after that three-thirty service. That was certainly the last time I would do that. I got the full experience. It was enough. I still had the orange from last night so there was no need to get out of bed. I would get yogurt from the dining room when I finally did rise.

Still, I was disappointed to have missed the Eucharist. I certainly never believed it was the actual body and blood of Christ, but I found it comforting, like the song we sang in Sunday school "Jesus Loves Me This I Know for The Bible Tells Me So." For me the Eucharist was about Jesus, not God. And I loved the idea that Jesus's last act was having a dinner party.

I rolled over and drifted back to sleep. A vision of the archbishop flashed through my head. God, he was attractive! However, not attractive enough to lose sleep over.

FITZ WAS ANTSY. The retreat was not what he had expected. He had thought he would be in a contemplative mood. But all he could contemplate was her. It was unlike him. He decided he had to get outside again, to not waste a precious second of this gorgeous day. He already loved the place. The expanse of it, the green, lush surroundings reminded him of Ireland—Glendalough, in particular. He walked down to the outdoor chapel. On his run he'd been in a hurry to get to breakfast. To see her. Now he could really explore.

The hay had been cut and was rolled up in bales along the road. The cattle, fenced in on the right, were grazing and lowing. There was a slight breeze rustling through the autumn leaves. A single tree had only changed half its colors. Blazing red on one side, green on the other. He couldn't help thinking of himself. Metanoia. He was clearly in the midst of changing his life. Going from green to red? Where would he end up? Red leaves turn brown, die and fall off the trees. Was that his future? He had come here with an open mind. He wanted to finally explore his feelings, something he had never really allowed himself to do.

After his mother and father had died, he shut himself off from his emotions. Only once had he let someone else in and that had caused him more pain than he had ever known in his life. He couldn't let that ever happen again. Yet he knew, with the trip to Italy looming, that he had to examine himself, his motivations, his desires, his intentions. He couldn't put it off any longer.

He stopped at the little open-air chapel, used for burials in the natural cemetery, a beautiful open slope facing down to the Shenandoah River. Simple river stones for headstones, engraved with the name and date of those who had died, dotted the meadow. They had not been embalmed, simply wrapped in shrouds and laid in the ground.

He sat on one of the wooden benches at the chapel with his back to the road, looking past the woods to the river, listening to its rushing waters. At first he hadn't noticed the stone. The enormous gray uneven-shaped river stone in the center of the chapel floor, clearly serving as some kind of altar. Their stone. The stone from

Glendalough. He couldn't bear it. The hurt came from deep within, propelling him off of the bench and out to the road. He slowly made his way back to the retreat house, lost in thought.

It was a few minutes before noon when he got back. Lunch time. He could hear the tinkle of the lunch bell as he entered the reception room. He glanced into the dining room. Empty. He stopped off in the men's room to collect himself. Would she be there?

I showed up late for lunch. Partly because I was luxuriating in bed, reading, sucking on my orange, and listening to Enya on my iPhone. Partly I was late because I was apprehensive about seeing the archbishop.

I had skipped Lauds and breakfast. I wondered if he had noticed. Probably not. He was a priest after all. An archbishop, actually. Surely he had loftier things to think about than a nervous, flaky middle-aged (*moi?*) woman.

I tried not to look for him as I came into the dining room, but I could see out of the corner of my eye that he was there. I could feel his presence. If I hadn't known better, I would have thought he was looking directly at me. I took my plate to serve myself and immediately dropped it on the table, causing a terrible clattering noise. Everyone stopped eating to look up. Dear Lord, this couldn't be happening. I spooned some roast pork, well-cooked green beans, and boiled potatoes on my plate. There was no room for salad and I didn't want to have to come back for it. I don't think I'd ever eaten that fast in my life. I gulped some water, quickly washed my plate, and disappeared before I could drop something else.

In my room, I dove back into my book of Greek mythology. I couldn't get enough of Pythia, the high priestess of the Temple of Apollo at Delphi, the oracle of Delphi. I felt a kinship with her because my mother, who also had a fascination with Pythia, named me Sybilla, meaning prophetess, sorceress. Although I've often had my psychic moments, I only wished now that I had more of her powers.

I skipped the two p.m. midday prayer. I was deep into my book and had made an appointment at two-thirty to meet with Father Joseph, the monk who was the counselor, the friend of Thomas Merton. I was misting up just thinking about whether I should tell him anything about Spraig or what, if anything, about my life. All I knew was, I had to tell someone.

I left my room at two twenty-five. When I opened the door, I glanced toward Fitz's room but realized he was probably at the chapel. The hallway was low-lit and empty. I paused in the reception to look at the bulletin board, stalling for time. I felt very apprehensive.

When I couldn't postpone it any longer, I headed down the hall to the left. The door was open into the small counseling room. A simple wooden table was set up with two chairs on either side facing each other. There were bookcases and a lamp and a carpeted floor. Perfect for meltdowns. As I walked in Father Joseph was seated behind the table and I recognized him as one of the monks I had seen at Lauds. He was the sweetest looking man I had ever seen. He looked much younger than his eighty-five years. His gray hair and bushy white eyebrows were set off by the color in his round face. His piercing blue eyes were all-knowing, all empathy, especially when he crinkled them. I loved his mouth with its tentative smile, almost waiting for the punch line of a joke. He got up and shut the door and beckoned me to sit. I took the chair that looked out the window at the lovely, weathering, weeping cherry tree. How apt. I had sworn to myself that I would not cry. I motioned to the tissues on the table.

"Ah," I joked. "The requisite box of Kleenex!"

Then I collapsed into tears.

I wasn't just upset about Spraig. I was horrified that I couldn't stop thinking about the archbishop. I was at the retreat to reflect on my marriage, and all I could focus on was James Fitzmaurice-Kelly. I couldn't even explain why, but I knew, sitting across from Father Joseph, that I was obsessed.

I had seen Fitz so many times on Spraig's show. I had read his books. So, I knew a lot about him. Before he was the archbishop, he'd been known as Fitz. He had read Yeats at Trinity College in Dublin. He was an international champion rugby player, the lead guitarist and singer in a rock band he started, The A.O.H. (for Ancient Order of Hibernians), and a licensed pilot. As archbishop, he was also well known in Dublin for his collection of motorcycles, motor scooters, and mountain bikes, embossed with large green shamrocks—the three-leaf clover representing the holy trinity, Father, Son, and Holy Ghost. Eschewing his car and driver he would zip around town, helmet askew, terrorizing the good ladies out for a walk on St. Stephen's Green. I knew the look on his face when he shook my husband's hand, and about his friendship with the late pope. But I hadn't known what it would be like to see him take over a room.

"I'm sorry to see that you're in so much pain," Father Joseph said.

"I'm sorry," I sputtered. "I promised myself I wouldn't cry."

"Don't worry, my dear. That's what the box of tissues is for, and we have plenty more." He pointed to the bookshelves, a pile of boxes in evidence. I couldn't help laughing.

When my weeping finally subsided, I sat there for a while, just trying to breathe. Father Joseph sat quietly. He didn't move.

"I'm Catholic, you know," I said, breaking the silence. Father Joseph said nothing. "Well, I was brought up Catholic. Actually, my mother is French Catholic. My father is a Boston WASP. I guess you could call me lapsed. I mean I don't go to Mass or anything. Some of the old habits and beliefs are familiar to me. I feel comfortable here. I should tell you that I'm pro-choice. The child sexual abuse scandal was enough to turn anyone away from the Church. The idea that women can't be priests is appalling. And the notion of mandatory celibacy I find unbelievably hypocritical." I waited to see if he would respond. I didn't want to be confrontational, but I felt it was important for him to know where I stood. He nodded. I wiped my eyes and my nose. "Anyway," I continued, "I just needed to talk to somebody who would understand. I'm married. I have been married for fifteen years." I twisted my gold wedding band with the fleur-de-lis engraving on it. "We're celebrating our fifteenth wedding anniversary soon. I say celebrating. It doesn't feel like much of a celebration to me."

"Why not?" Father Joseph asked.

"Well, because . . ." I started to cry again. "Our marriage is in trouble."

"Tell me about it," he said.

I MET SPRAIG AT A REHEARSAL dinner for mutual friends on the upper side of New York. I had been stunned when he walked in the door.

I remember whispering to a friend, "Who's the Viking?" And her saying, "Forget it. Every girl in New York is after him." I couldn't keep my eyes off him. I watched him as he walked around the room greeting friends. He was so at ease, so sure of himself. To my surprise I could see he was casually working his way over to me. He stopped as he got to where I was standing, holding my glass of champagne, and pretending I hadn't noticed him.

"I must know you," he said, fully confident that I must feel the same way. "What is your name?"

"Sybilla," I answered.

"A sorceress! I'm in trouble. If I get you another glass of champagne, Sybilla, will you promise not to put a spell on me?"

"You'll have to take your chances," I said to him. I couldn't believe I was so cool. "Besides, I don't even know your name. I can't very well put a spell on you if I don't know who you are."

"Spraig," he said, laughing.

"Oh, Spraig, you're easy. You don't stand a chance."

We left together that evening. I spent the night with him. We were engaged in less than six months and married within a year. I didn't have a doubt in my mind.

Those first few years were a fantasy. We both worked hard. I had worked for *The Harvard Crimson*, the Harvard newspaper, and also wrote for the *Harvard Review* where I eventually got a job as a junior editor. Spraig had studied politics and foreign policy and began writing for *Foreign Affairs Magazine* as a very young member of the Council on Foreign Relations. At the council he had begun doing interviews with foreign policy experts for meetings and was so good that he became a regular on cable news. We traveled a lot, we had many friends and an active social life, we had an adorable apartment at East 75th and Lexington. The most important thing was that he treated me like a queen. He was devoted and loving. He was gentle and tender. We had a great sex life. He talked a lot about our future, how he wanted children, my children, and what a wonderful family we would be. I really felt cherished. We were happy. It was all too good to be true.

As it turned out, that was right. Certainly, there were things I didn't admire about him, things I had a difficult time overlooking. I didn't like the way he talked to waiters and taxi drivers and people he thought were less important than he was. There was an imperiousness about him, a sense of entitlement. Politically, he was to the right of me. Most of the time we could agree to disagree but sometimes on social issues I found it difficult. We also didn't like the same things.

My parents had a house on the beach in Martha's Vineyard. They had a key to South Beach, the most beautiful beach on the island. They had bought the house for $35,000 a hundred years ago. It was now worth about half a million dollars. I loved going there. Spraig didn't. He thought it was too low-key. No fancy shops or restaurants, no celebrities anyone ever sees.

He preferred Southampton, New York with its fancy mansions and black tie charity dinners, Maseratis, Palm Beach overtones, and money money money.

He finally got into the Meadow Club after waiting for five years and you would have thought he had won the Nobel prize. He was particularly proud of the grass stains on his tennis shoes as the Meadow Club has grass courts, a rarity anywhere.

I loathed Southampton. Spraig knew it. It was everything I didn't want in a summer vacation. I had friends in other parts of the Hamptons, mostly writers and journalists, but had no desire to spend any time there. Spraig couldn't wait until he made enough money to buy in Southampton, which he promptly did, as a "surprise" for me, when he got his big prime-time talk show.

A year later, he joined the Racquet Club in New York so he could play squash in the winter. I am not a club person. I've never belonged to a club in my life. I see most clubs as just another way to keep people out, to make yourself feel superior. The only sort of club I ever liked is the so-called "Yacht Club" on the Vineyard: a funky spruced up shack with wooden tables and benches on the back porch overlooking the rocky beach. Members, if they're lucky, can get a BLT or a grilled cheese. It has two things going for it: access to the water and tennis courts—which most people on the Vineyard, even really rich ones, don't have.

One thing Spraig and I did agree on was Italy. We both loved Italy. But his Italy was different from mine. I adored the little hill towns in Tuscany, driving from one small hotel to another, tasting wines, swimming in the sea, discovering out-of-the-way family restaurants where the pasta was delectable and the wine recently stomped on by the local villagers. After Spraig and I got together he only wanted to go to the posh places. The Amalfi Coast, Positano, Capri, Porto Ercole, Portofino. Only five-star hotels, where I insisted we always get the cheapest room. He was drawn to the glitterati. When he started making a name for himself, we began getting invitations to various boondoggles. Yacht owners always need sparkling guests to entertain them. They never lack for plenty. The bigger the yacht the more twinkly the stars. We got invited to tour the coast of Italy on a mega yacht owned by a big donor to the Council on Foreign Relations.

We had a huge stateroom—our luggage was unpacked for us. There were elaborate meals cooked by a French chef, shopping trips taken by launch, crew members to carry our bags, swimming in the boat's pool, flying to and from the airport on the yacht's helicopter. The saving grace of the trip was the captain, who knew every yacht at every port and every port was dotted, or rather splotched, by them. He could recite the names of the owners, mostly Russian oligarchs and other shady characters, as well as a litany of malfeasance, like which ones had their mistresses on board instead of their wives. It was delicious. At one island we had to go through a narrow passage between cliffs to get to the town's harbor, which was subsumed by our vessel. When we disembarked, the boat was surrounded by onlookers staring, or glaring, at us. It wasn't clear whether it was out of curiosity, admiration, or contempt. I wanted to shout out, "No, No! You don't understand. I'm not one of THOSE people." But there I was. Spraig thought he had died and gone to heaven.

Then there was Greece. The island of Spetses, the most magical place I had ever been. The one spot, no matter what else was happening in my life, where I was always truly happy. My grandparents had a house on Spetses since my mother was growing up. It was on a bluff in the Old Harbor, overlooking the sea and the islands, Hydra in the mist. It was a family compound at the end of a long dirt road. We got around by Vespa: me driving, Spraig in the back.

My mother's sister Delphine has the house next door, separated only by a wall. The houses were old and not really decorated, like the Vineyard, just comfortable and easy but beautiful in the simple Greek way. Lots of faded blues and whites, bougainvillea climbing everywhere and a grove of fig trees, olive trees, and pomegranate trees all over the unmanicured gardens. We even had a small amphitheater on the property. The family built a tiny chapel next door where we have weddings and christenings and funerals. We swam off the rocks below every day and occasionally rented a *kaiki*, an open-air boat, to go around the island, stopping off for picnics or at little tavernas on the beaches.

Spraig couldn't stand Greece. It was too hot. There was no tennis or golf. He got seasick and hates boats—other than the yachts. All of our friends there were either French or Greek. Most of them didn't really know what a big star he was. He didn't like Greek people. He didn't like Greek food either. He found it unimaginative.

I had always dreamed of getting married at this little chapel in Spetses. But Spraig refused, so we got married in Boston. Which was fine with me. I was so in love I would have gotten married anywhere he wanted. And besides, I always knew I would insist that our children be christened on Spetses. That was enough for me.

I spent an hour telling Father Joseph everything: about Spraig, about my life, about Spetses. He listened intently. Once I had stopped crying, talking to him became easier and I realized I couldn't stop. I had no idea whether Father Joseph knew who Spraig was or who I was. I couldn't imagine this eighty-five-year-old monk hanging around the monastery watching TV.

I also had no idea how he was responding to my story. He seemed entirely sympathetic, yet I hoped he didn't think that I was entitled.

I hadn't meant to prattle on. It was just that the spigot was open, and it wouldn't shut off. I couldn't any more have quit talking than I could have quit breathing.

"I'm sorry," I said, after an hour. "I'm talking too much."

"You're just warming up," Father Joseph said, shaking his head.

"You must think I'm the most spoiled, self-centered, privileged little brat you've ever met. I'm embarrassed by me." Before he could say anything, I kept on. "I just listened to myself. One extraordinary opportunity and gift after another has been bestowed upon me. All of my life I've had everything. Nobody could have wanted more. When I think of the grief and sadness and pain in the world, the vivid images I can't erase from my mind of babies being bayoneted in their mother's arms and thrown live into a burning fire, I can't begin to compare my sorrow with theirs. I have no right to feel sorry for myself. How dare I complain because my husband drags me on yachts, buys fancy houses, doesn't like my watering holes. I make myself sick. Every morning I wake up and start feeling depressed and then I force myself to say a prayer of gratitude. I know that's become a cliche. But I'm always so aware of my good fortune that I feel guilty even having a twinge of distress. When I think of my pitiful little problems compared to others I'm consumed with shame. If ever I find myself saying 'why me?' I say, 'why not me?' And yet . . . and yet there are times when I feel in such deep despair that I really don't want to go on living anymore." I shifted in my chair, wiping my cheeks with a tissue. "It's a conundrum for me. I have such a capacity for love, for caring, for cherishing. I have nobody to cherish anymore and nobody to cherish me. That's all I want, really. To be loved."

I continued weeping. Not wracking sobs this time. It was more out of resignation than anything. The wetness made my eyes blurry. Through my lashes, I saw Father Joseph rub his chin.

"You know, Sybilla, the world is full of suffering," he said. "Who's to say yours is not as valid as another's. We all suffer. Nobody gets a pass. Now if it were Spraig sitting here complaining about how you didn't like yachts and the glitterati and Southampton I would have a different view. But I would see someone who is suffering terribly as well. Do you believe in God?"

"I don't know what that means," I said. "I don't know what or who God is. I do feel a connection to the divine, if that's what you're talking about. But everyone has a different idea of God."

"What's yours?"

I thought for a while.

"I've studied religion, I've thought a lot about it. I've accepted God at one point and rejected him, her, it. I've prayed, not prayed, not believed in God, been angry with God. Yet how can you be angry with a God you don't believe in? Jesus is an entirely different story. I can't get my head around Jesus. I've longed for God. I've been desolate without God. I've wrestled with the question of God, sometimes until it makes me crazy. I have wanted to believe. It seems people are happier when they believe. It would be such a relief to be able to say, 'It's God's will' and accept the pain and suffering. I would love to just put everything in God's hands, and say, 'There, you take it on.' But I can't. It doesn't work for me. When I try to pray, I don't quite know how or for what. Should I pray for world peace? How about people all over the world who live in anguish, sick and starving and in danger. Do I pray for them? Do I pray for myself, for my marriage? And does God say, 'Sure, Sybilla, I'll take care of your problems, screw the others?' I don't understand petitionary prayer. Two football teams in opposite locker rooms praying to the same God to let them win? How does God know who to choose? Two politicians running against each other, both on their knees to God. It makes no sense to me. People often ask me if I'm an atheist. I used to say yes but then I thought that was a negative way to look at life. I don't deny there is a God. But agnostic means nothing to me. We're all agnostic. Nobody really knows. The pope is an agnostic. Forgive me. He believes but he doesn't *know* know."

Father Joseph burst out laughing and crossed himself.

"You still didn't answer my question," he said.

"Do I believe in God?" I smiled. "You don't give up do you?"

"That's why I'm paid the big bucks."

"What's that song, 'I Believe'? 'Every time I hear a newborn baby cry, or touch a leaf, or see the sky, then I know why, I believe.'" My voice got shakier. "We can't have children." I could barely speak. "Spraig is infertile. I'm thirty-nine years old. I'm in a dead marriage and my husband is infertile."

"Now I understand," Father Joseph said. We were both silent for a moment. "I think," he added, "this is a good place to take a break before five-thirty Vespers. I can see you again on Thursday if you like."

"I like," I said.

AFTER LUNCH, Fitz walked down to the outdoor chapel and turned left toward the Shenandoah. He passed the Scattering Garden, its yellow wildflowers at the end of their season like those buried in the natural graveyard sloping toward the river. He admired the simple river stones with names etched on them, one in Arabic. There was an old, dilapidated barn, gray with age and neglect, the hay silo, hanging on to its side for dear life held up only by desperately clinging vines. The barn was once the proud occupant of the riverbank. How beautiful it must have been, how peaceful, to have sat on the open side of the barn on one of the now rotting picnic tables and listened to the water as it swept its way past the forgotten timbers. He followed the path through the weeds down to the edge of the river and saw that it continued quite a way to the right. Looking at the curve, nostalgia overtook him. He was back in Glendalough by the Lugduff Brook, the water flowing into the upper lake where he had fallen in love once before. Here was their rock, this one not as smooth as the one in the open-air chapel but rougher and more jagged, jutting its way out into the water. In Glendalough, they would take off their shoes and sit there, dangling their feet, laughing as it cooled and tickled their toes. Here was their tree, almost dead, leaning out into the river like the Tower of Pisa on the verge of collapse. Its roots had been unearthed and were barely clutching the ground, determined not to fall over. The roots were old and ugly and twisted, yet they had a noble resolve not to give in, not to give up, not to succumb. Fitz was repelled by the tree, by the jumbled squirming roots. It made him sad and afraid. It reminded him somehow of his childhood. Yet through the fallen auburn leaves surrounding it there was a tiny patch of dappled sunlight. Could it be his imagination that the birds' nest in the tree was shaped like a heart? He didn't know. He had an urge to jump into the river and just keep swimming, wash his sins away, drown himself. Instead, he turned away from the tree and walked back down the path toward the barn.

He was hoping Sybilla would show up at Vespers, but she didn't. On some level, he was relieved. He felt an odd sense of guilt and confusion when she was around, but even without her there, he had a hard time concentrating.

The others seemed deep in prayer. He forgot to cross himself. As soon as it was over he raced back down to the retreat house so as not to be late for dinner. They were all coming into the dining room at the same time. She wasn't there. He went to get his plate from the counter, not even paying attention to what he put on it. He took his seat and began eating distractedly. Sausage and sauerkraut casserole with noodles and cheese. Interesting. Apple sauce, salad, bread, and the leftover dessert from lunch. Apple crumble. He wasn't really hungry. He had eaten too much of the pork. He took a sip of water and looked up. There she was. She was looking right at him but quickly glanced away. Her hair was brushed slightly toward her face, falling over one eye and she was wearing tinted glasses. Her nose was pink. Was she sick? She had on black yoga pants and a long-sleeved white T-shirt. Her shoulders were slightly hunched over. She looked depleted. She looked the way he felt. She got her plate and rushed through the meal. They both pushed their chairs away from the table to get up at the same time. She left quickly, out into the hall and down the stairs to her room before he got to his. She shut the door behind her. He wondered if she would make it to Compline. He knew he had to go. He was desperately in need of beseeching.

I came back from dinner completely wrung out. I hadn't recovered at all from my session with Father Joseph. I sank into the mattress and buried my face in the pillow. I had had no intention of spilling out the detritus of my life. It was all so shambolic. Now that I had started to let it out, I didn't want to stop. The compulsion to go knock on Father Joseph's door, drag him back to the consultation room and finish my pitiful story was almost uncontrollable. At least I would get to see him again on Thursday.

I hadn't told him everything about Spraig. After Spraig had found out he couldn't procreate his whole personality changed and so did his attitude toward me. He became someone I didn't know. We went to a shrink. It was a disaster and he quit after three sessions. He was angry and hostile, and he took it out on me. I understood how painful, devastating really, it must have been for him. I knew how much he wanted children, a family. I tried to be sympathetic. I tried to tell him it was alright. Of course it wasn't alright. I was destroyed by the news. I wanted children terribly. I was heartbroken. I was desperate. I tried to bring up adoption, even a sperm donor. He went berserk. He was Spraig Oglethorpe Exley. His child would be his or nobody's. The most hurtful thing was that he never said he was sorry for me, that he knew what pain I must have been in, that it was my loss as well. It seemed as if it was all about him and his manhood. It was about his bloody ego. It wasn't my fault. It wasn't my fault, I kept crying to him, but he had to blame somebody and that somebody was me. It was by far the most difficult thing I have ever gone through in my otherwise "perfect" little life. The "excellent young Exleys" weren't young or excellent anymore.

I could hear the bell tolling for Compline. The sun had already set behind the hills. I debated not going but something compelled me to get up, put on my shoes, brush my hair, grab a flashlight, and get out the door.

I had to have the peace, the solace, the silence of Compline. I wanted the candles, the chanting, the praying. I needed the darkness, the mystery. I yearned to fall on my knees in supplication. To whom, to what, I did not know.

He was there in his usual spot in the second row all the way to the left. We hadn't been asked to sit in the same seats, as we were at dinner, but somehow we took our rightful places. The others were all there. Each one of them had clearly experienced something life-changing already. You could see it in their posture and in their expressions.

Fitz's head and shoulders were bowed. The monks began to emerge from their lodging, quietly sitting, one and then another after bowing to the cross. We sat when they prayed and stood when they chanted. I closed my eyes and breathed deeply. Inhale, exhale. Inhale, exhale. My body relaxed. I was embraced by the solitude. I was on another plane. Then it was over. My eyes were still shut tight. I could vaguely hear the monks retreating, then the others quietly leaving as well. I could tell his footsteps. He paused slightly before he closed the door. I felt him looking at me, wondering if I was okay. At last, I came to. My flashlight was in my jacket pocket so as not to forget it. The cool evening air hit me in the face as I closed the chapel door behind me. In the distance I saw that he was lagging behind the others. I knew he wanted to make sure I didn't need his help. I switched on the flashlight and started walking. He picked up his pace when he heard me. He was back at the house and had disappeared into his room by the time I got there. I was relieved. I didn't want him to see what a mess I was.

I really could have used a long soak in a deep tub, but a hot shower would have to do. I toweled myself off and wrapped up in my beige cashmere sweats Maman had given me years ago for Christmas. They were the coziest things I owned, my security blanket. When I was feeling really depressed, I would curl up on the bed in them, put on some fuzzy socks, snuggle up against my myriad down pillows and just disappear. That's exactly what I did. I picked up my book of Greek mythology but couldn't get into Achilles and Briseis. I had brought along the unicorn needlepoint pillow I was working on. Nothing relaxed me more than doing needlework. It was my great escape. I reached in my bag and brought it out, threaded the needle and began to stitch. What I hadn't expected that night was that the unicorn on the canvas would make me so sad. Pure white, he was sitting gracefully in a tiny enclosure, completely surrounded by a small wooden fence which allowed him only enough room to stand. His graceful front legs sprawled out in front of him, the hind legs beneath him. His lovely ivory tail curled up toward the fence like a puff of smoke. His proud head was held high, facing to one side, a wisp of beard tumbled from his chin, his piercing single long alabaster swirled horn pointing up to the sky. Around his neck was a wide black and gold bejeweled belt. He was in a calm posture, one of surrender. It was his eye that I found so arresting. It was deep and black and somewhat bewildered. He was surrounded by an exquisite garden, replete with colorful flowers and there was a large tree growing inside the fence which was entwined with a rope spelling out the letters AD. I kept going back to his eye. It would be the last thing on the canvas I would sew. If I could stand it. I knew in my soul why he seemed bewildered, confused. It was as if he were saying, "My God, My God, Why hast thou forsaken me?" I peered at the needlepoint, inexorably drawn to the unicorn as a symbol of imagery, mythology, and Christology.

At around ten-thirty I heard the strains of a guitar coming from the hallway. I wondered if someone had turned on the sound system. It was beautiful, haunting music. I put down my needlepoint, crept to my door and cracked it open to listen. It was coming from Fitz's room. Of course. He had had a guitar with him when he arrived. He was humming a melody along with his playing and I recognized the song at once. It was Bono. My favorite. "I Still Haven't Found What I'm Looking For." His voice ladened with grief. I left the door ajar and went back to my bed, turned out the light, pulled the covers over my head, and lay there in silence, transported. His grief was catching. I mouthed the words to the song, "I have climbed highest mountains, I have run through the fields, only to be with you, I have run, I have crawled, I have scaled these city walls, these city walls, only to be with you. But I still haven't found what I'm looking for. But I still haven't found what I'm looking for."

Before I knew it, I had been plunged back into the anguish of my day. I couldn't stay in my room alone. Without even thinking, I got up and walked out of my room to the chapel. The door was shut. It was empty. I was still alone. Only one candle was burning and a pale light over the altar shone down on the cross. The table-high, stone holy water receptacle greeted me as I entered. Instinctively I dipped my fingers in and crossed my forehead.

I could still hear the thrumming of his guitar. I walked over to the wall, looking for something to distract me. There hung a large wooden cross, Jesus firmly nailed to it. Blood was streaming out of his hands and his feet, his knees and his side. The crown of thorns dug deeply into his head and blood gushed from that too. His torso was swathed in a golden cloth. I was repulsed. How could anyone possibly believe in a loving God who would do that to his own son? More than that, how could anyone possibly worship a monstrous God who would commit such a heinous act. It was unfathomable to me. I thought of Spraig. As an atheist he was the voice of reason. Then I thought of Fitz. He had devoted his whole life to this God. Which one was the better person? There was no contest. I was overpowered by confusion. I started to leave, but something held me back.

I turned around and looked to the right of the altar. There was the Virgin Mary, draped in red, cradling her baby, arms wrapped around his tiny swaddling. A song reverberated in my head, "Mary, Did You Know?" She couldn't have known. She looked too serene. I realized I was envious of Mary, even though she was to lose her only child in the most gruesome way. I was envious of her because she had a child and I didn't. What heresy from a good Catholic girl, a good Catholic girl who had said countless novenas to her over the years. I instinctively crossed myself. I would do it again. I would beg for her grace. One last time. I had no choice. I fell to my knees on the soft carpet before the altar. "Blessed Mary, Mother of God," I began, but I couldn't go on. I was filled with even more self-loathing than I had been with Father Joseph. Unable to control my emotions I bent over, my head practically touching the floor as I clutched my empty womb, heaving with sobs.

I heard footsteps behind me. Before I realized what was happening Fitz had lifted me off of the floor and enfolded me in his arms. He held me for the longest time, rocking me back and forth. My tears subsided. He pulled a handkerchief out of his pocket and wiped them away. Then he began to stroke my hair, so gentle, so soothing. I can't say how long we stood there, wrapped around each other, I clinging to him as hard as he to me. I didn't remember ever being anywhere else.

"Sybilla," he whispered, almost inaudibly. "Sybilla."

At last, I was calm. He could feel me relax. His arms loosened around me. I pulled slightly apart and looked up at him. His eyes were piercing. I didn't look away. He let me go. I backed off slightly. He stood in front of me for a moment, then turned and silently walked away through the door to his room.

Wednesday

Fitz didn't sleep well. He thrashed about in his sheets, his body roiling as much as his mind. He had come to the monastery to contemplate his life in the Church, his role as a priest, his future under the new pope. Now he found himself in a liminal state, unable to concentrate on what had brought him here, obsessed by someone who had appeared out of nowhere. He believed God had brought Sybilla to the abbey to test his faith. It was so unexpected, so confounding.

He couldn't wait to get to Lauds at seven. He rolled out of bed, put on his gray sweats and sneakers and dashed up the hill to the chapel, not waiting for the bells to toll. He felt almost as if he were on his way to an urgent meeting. He had to hash it out with God, needed to have a confrontation.

He was the first one there. He headed for his usual place to the left in the second row, bowing and crossing himself as he approached the altar. The monks hadn't even come yet. He knelt.

"Dear God," he said under his breath. "What are you doing to me? I have been so secure in your love and in my love for you. Perhaps I have been smug, but I have never doubted. The Church yes. I sometimes feel the Church is a perversion of all you have given us, a perversion of all that Jesus has wanted for us. I have given my life to you. It's true I have been distracted from your work because of my own but only because I feel as if you are being misrepresented and I needed to speak out. I came here to find peace. To spend time alone with you. To be silent. I felt as if I had begun to lose our connection with each other. Yet, the publicity, the adulation, the TV shows, the excellent book reviews, all seemed to me to be a validation of what you wanted me to do. Still, there has been a distance. And now I'm here with you and you have thrown an obstacle between us. What am I to make of Sybilla and my ardent feelings for her? Cacoethes. The Greeks said it best. I have an irresistible urge to do something inadvisable. I can only believe that this is your doing. But why? What is your message? Do you want to test me, to see if you are still the only vessel of my wonder and awe? Or do you want me to break my vows? Or are you punishing me for having broken them once? Dear God, I pray to you. Please help me to understand. I will surrender to your will. But I must know what it is. Guide me oh, Lord. In Jesus's name. Amen."

He had been so deep in prayer that he hadn't even noticed that the monks had come in, that others had arrived and were sitting behind him. The chanting was coming to an end. He was still on his knees. He found himself shaking. The praying hadn't worked this time. He needed, he realized, to go for a run. He often found clarity while running. He stood and left the chapel before the service was over, grateful she had not shown up.

Once outside, he took off to the end of the drive and out onto the main road. He flew down the country lane past the farmhouses. He was so steeped in adrenaline he felt he was almost levitating.

At one point he glanced at his watch, only just remembering that he had a ten a.m. session with Father Joseph. He turned around and headed back to the guest house, making it a little after nine. He was pouring with sweat and went immediately to his room where he stripped, jumped into the hot shower and lathered himself from head to toe. It was cleansing in more ways than one. He was trying to scrub away his confusion, get back to being himself.

After he had dried off, he combed through his thick curly hair. It made him smile to remember his mother, slicking back his wet hair after a bath and telling him what a handsome boyo he was. Back in his jeans and a black cotton crew neck pullover he went upstairs to get something to eat. The dining room was empty. He poured himself some cheerios with milk and cut up a banana. He ate quickly, retrieved a couple of hard-boiled eggs, a few pieces of wheat bread, and an apple for later and went back to his room to get his notebook. He had to collect himself, gather his thoughts. He didn't want to digress. He wanted to get to the point with Father Joseph. Actually, he was rather looking forward to their conversation. He didn't know what he was in for.

I DIDN'T WAKE UP UNTIL TEN. I had stumbled back to my room, a quivering mess from my encounter with Fitz, beyond exhausted from my emotionally tumultuous day and tumbled into bed, barely able to turn out the light. I remembered nothing until I opened one eye and checked my phone for the time. I was shocked. I couldn't remember having slept that soundly since I was a teenager. I felt rested for the first time in ages. I yawned and stretched and curled up around my pillow to daydream a little before I finally allowed myself to be fully awake. Then it all came trickling back into my brain. Fitz holding me, kissing my head, stroking my hair, whispering my name. I had wrapped my arms around his waist. He had rocked me back and forth. I hadn't wanted to ever let him go. We had stood that way for what seemed an eternity. I could tell he hadn't wanted to let me go either. Finally, we had silently, reluctantly pulled apart, an unspoken agreement that we had to. We looked at each other with longing. It was even harder to break away from each other's astonished gazes. I knew if he hadn't turned and walked away I would have fallen back into his arms.

Now I squeezed the pillow and tried to examine my feelings. I was reeling. Where to begin? About Fitz. My attraction to him was all-consuming. We had never spoken, apart from when he'd whispered my name, but I knew he had a deep resonant voice from seeing him on TV. I hadn't ever felt so drawn to anyone in my life. Intellectually, I certainly knew him. Physically I had only seen him—well, embraced him. Yes, he was gorgeous. Spiritually I could only imagine. Emotionally? I saw that last night. He had been unbridled. I had the feeling that it was not a familiar experience for him.

It was his emotions that took over and completely undid me. That I would never have expected. I had read once an article about twin flames. Two people who are destined to be together, beings that help our souls find completion. Plato's idea of souls split in two. The experience of finding one's twin flame could be terrifying, overwhelming, and disorienting. I wondered if Fitz was mine. The definition certainly fit. I knew then that he would play an extremely important role in my life. I hadn't expected the "wonder, joy, anxiety, and intoxication" the article talked about. It hadn't mentioned lust. It was actually intense sexual desire, almost lasciviousness that I felt for him. I craved him. I had to have him.

I moaned and rolled over clutching my gut. It had been months, maybe even a year since Spraig and I had had sex. More and more he was pulling away from me. I understood. He was clearly ashamed of not being able to give me a child. That was probably the reason, psychologically, why I had lost all sexual attraction for him. Still, I would love to be held. Even that he couldn't give me. I was climbing the walls. I needed to get laid. I had actually contemplated having an affair, but I had never been attracted to anyone before Fitz. Just the thought of all that sneaking around and lying made me tired. Even though that was what Spraig had been doing. I just hadn't wanted to know.

Happily, I had brought along my trusty vibrator. These days I went nowhere without it, or rather "him." I had bought one about two years ago surreptitiously while in a different neighborhood when Spraig first learned that he was infertile and our sex life went south. It was a small gray three-speeder. Not great but did the trick. I named him Jean-Jean after a very sexy French boyfriend I had once had at the Sorbonne. After a year or so of virtually no sex I realized I needed something more satisfying. I went back to the same drug store. I couldn't find the damn vibrators and finally had to ask the saleslady, a Muslim woman in a hijab. I approached her in the packed store and quietly asked if they had vibrators. She had no idea what I was talking about. Before I could stop her, she had turned to the guy at the front counter and said in a loud voice, "Do we have vibrators?" Suddenly a thousand eyes were on me, a thousand smirks on people's lips. I nearly died. "Over there"—he pointed in a loud voice—"are the vibrators," making sure everyone heard. Alone at last, I picked out the biggest one in the store, a shocking pink number with twelve speeds and a little pink extension. I grabbed it, went to the self-pay machine, struggled to figure out how to work it (I certainly wasn't going to ask for help) and made a hasty exit. "Grand Jean" had gotten me through the past year and a half.

Now I reached for him again. This time I barely had to touch myself before I exploded. Fitz. How was I ever going to stay away from you?

I lay there for a bit, luxuriating in the feeling of being satisfied, or at least somewhat satisfied. My phone pinged. I looked at the screen. It was Spraig, texting me.

"I miss you," the message read.

Very un-Spraig. He never said anything like that. But then I had never gone away like this, left him alone, unless it was for an assignment or to visit my parents. He didn't understand it. Not just the monastery thing but the fact that I needed to get away from him which was obvious. He was scared. Maybe he saw that there had been a tipping point. That the sarcasm, venom, contempt and anger he had been directing at me had suddenly pushed me over the edge. I didn't respond immediately. Another ping.

"Can we talk?"

I don't know why but I suddenly felt horribly guilty as if I had done something wrong.

"This is a SILENT retreat," I texted. "We'll talk when I get back."

"Sybilla, I have a good mind to drive down there and drag you out of this cult before you have to be deprogrammed."

"Then you'd better bring two thugs and a straitjacket because I am going nowhere."

He didn't respond.

The bell rang. It was lunch time. I got out of bed and put on a light shift and my walking sandals. I looked in the mirror. My face was flushed from my encounter with Grand Jean. I put on a little lipstick, ran a brush through my hair and went upstairs. I was practically hyperventilating at the thought of seeing him.

FITZ MADE HIS WAY apprehensively up the stairs and down the hall to the consultation room. Father Joseph rose to greet him as he entered. "Your Grace," he said with a slight bow.

"Please, Father. I'm not Your Grace here. I'm Fitz." Father Joseph got up to shut the door behind Fitz and motioned him to the chair facing the window. "That will be hard for me," Father Joseph said.

"I'm sure you can handle it," replied Fitz with a laugh.

He took a moment to glance around the room and was comforted by the ambiance. It was cozy and welcoming, a safe place to confide. The walls lined with bookshelves, the carpeted floor, the soft lighting, and the view of the meadows was reminiscent of the space he had created for himself in his office in Dublin. He smiled at the box of tissues on the table between him and Father Joseph. He always kept a box of tissues in every room of his house and at the office too. It was almost inevitable that those who came to seek his advice, wisdom, counseling, approval, remonstrances, consolation, would break down at some point. Thank God he wouldn't need them today. They sat for a moment in silence. Father Joseph waited for Fitz to speak. Fitz moved uneasily in his chair. He would wait him out. Or maybe not.

"What's going on in your prayers?" asked Father Joseph.

It took Fitz by surprise. He had absolutely no idea what to say.

"I, well, I—I've been so exhausted lately, so distracted . . . I've had trouble reaching out to God, if you want the truth." He was immediately sorry he had said that. "What I mean is . . ."

"No need to explain. This is not a test. There are no rules here. You are here because you are searching. So are we all. Everyone does it in their own way. Enjoy God's creation. Notice what comes. Take the first days and relax. Pray to God and nature." Fitz could feel the tension leaving his body. "God asks, 'Is anyone thirsty? Come and drink.' This is a great day. God has invited you to a space of calm and peace."

"Thank you," Fitz said. "Thank you." There was a comfortable pause. Fitz broke it by saying, "So, I understand you knew Thomas Merton."

"Yes," Father Joseph said, and his face lit up.

"I never had the honor of meeting him, but I admired him enormously. I've read almost everything he wrote. He was quite the fellow."

"That he was."

"He's gone to glory."

"As well he should."

"I've always identified with him. We got off to the same start. He and I," continued Fitz, "had similar childhoods. Our parents both died at an early age. We were both raised by relatives. We were both wild in our early years. What saved me was Yeats. I had one great teacher who introduced me to Yeats, to his spirituality and his mysticism. It spoke to me more than religion ever had."

Father Joseph nodded. It seemed to Fitz as though he understood all too well what Fitz was saying. Fitz was playing for time. He knew, at some point, he was going to have to talk about it. About her. But he wasn't ready yet.

"I took pilgrimages during weekends in Sligo where I sat by Yeats's tomb in the churchyard, walked the hills where he walked, drank in the places he drank. If they had been alive, I would have slept with the women he slept with."

That elicited a chuckle.

"As a teenager and then as a young man I continued to read Yeats. I felt a calling. I didn't know to what, but it was compelling. My professor at Trinity sensed my passion for the poet and even though my marks were terrible he got me into a PhD program where I studied Yeats. I wanted to really ponder who Yeats was and what he was about. Yes, yes, everyone knew he was a brilliant poet. He was also known as a bit of a kook. The whole occult thing, you know." Father Joseph nodded. "Even Auden taunted him a bit in his 'In Memory of W.B. Yeats.' 'You were silly like us; your gift survived it all' . . . But it was Maude Gonne who gave him the sobriquet 'Silly Billy,' not necessarily to his amusement. In the end, though, I concluded that he wasn't silly at all. He believed that there was another world, that all of our individual minds are in some way connected to that world and that we create symbols for those worlds. That sounds like God to me. It worked for him. It works for me. It got him where he wanted to go with his beliefs. That's more than most of us can say. Except maybe Frank Sinatra."

Father Joseph laughed.

"Yeats turned my life around," Fitz continued. "It was his Spiritus Mundi that provided me with inspiration and a sense of the collective unconscious. I came to see that so much of what seemed to be secular in Yeats's writing was really sacred. I think he was a deeply religious man. His poetry was his way of speaking to God, of expressing his beliefs. He was supremely pluralistic. He was generous with his spirituality and his acceptance of the many different kinds of thought. He was ahead of his time. 'Everything that man esteems endures a moment or a day.' He understood that nobody believes exactly the same thing."

"You can say that again," Father Joseph chortled.

"He was adventurous in his faith, no coward he."

"He was certainly not averse to trying new ideas."

"Or new ways to reach transcendence. I understand why some people ridiculed him for his forays into the occult and magic. But tell me Father, if religion is not magical, if the belief in God is not magical, if Jesus Christ is not magical then what is? Yeats experimented with drugs, or as his life-long love, Maude Gonne, called it, 'white powder.' I did the same while I was getting my degree. As so many religions have done for thousands of years and still do today. I had epiphanies and moments of transcendence . . . Each one brought me closer to God. 'For one throb of the artery . . . I knew that One is animate.'" He paused, smiled a little sheepishly. "Sorry for the lecture, Father. And about the white powder. Some of my friends at Trinity may well have described my 'religious experimentation' as being stoned out of my mind half the time."

Father Joseph smiled back. "It seems to have done the trick."

"Aye, that it did."

"So, what was it that finally drew you to the priesthood?

"I wasn't ready to sail to Byzantium."

"And?" Father Joseph said.

"And what?"

Father Joseph stood to open a window and said with his back to Fitz, "Is it what you've wanted?"

"I considered being a monk. But I didn't get the call. I have felt that it's a terrible shortcoming. When I do something, I want to do it right, do it completely. I don't ever go halfway. But the monastic life! It was too much for me. I couldn't see myself living that way. So I justified my choice by saying that I wanted to be out in the world, helping people, doing good. Partly that's true. But the fact is I didn't have the devotion to our God to give myself to him completely. I didn't have the courage. For that I am ashamed." Father Joseph returned to his seat but didn't speak. "There's a quote from Merton that sticks in my mind. I roll it around in my brain when I'm trying to decide who I want to be at this late date, still wondering in what direction I should go. I'm sure you know the quote. 'This is a true and special vocation. There are few who are willing to belong completely to such silence, to let it soak into their bones, to breathe nothing but silence, to feed on silence, and to turn the very substance of their life into a living and vigilant silence.' Perhaps that's what drew me here. To be in silence for a week. To see what it feels like, to contemplate the possibility of living this way for the rest of my life."

Father Joseph leaned forward on his elbows, his hands clasped in front of him, his eyes looking directly into Fitz's.

"Fitz," he said. "If I may. Why are you really here?"

One tear, then another splashed down Fitz's angular face. His already sloping eyebrows, that suggested melancholy and empathy at the same time, turned downward. Suddenly his face was awash, wet with pain, anguish really, raw grief.

"I have sinned."

"We are not here to talk about sin. This is not confession. The priest is coming tomorrow for that. You can have at it with him."

"But sin is part of the story."

"Actually, I think love is the story here. Love and a broken heart. You know the Japanese have a word for it. *Takotsubo*. Broken heart syndrome. You can't hide it. You put up a good front, but it's written all over you."

"Dierdre," he said finally. "I'm here because of Dierdre. Deirdre of the sorrows."

When Fitz first met Dierdre he was already a priest in Dublin. She was a nun and a schoolteacher. He had come to visit the school as he did on his rounds through the parishes.

He was taken by her immediately. She had pale hair and pale blue eyes and pale alabaster skin. She was so delicate, so ethereal and as beautiful inside as out. She looked like the exquisite maiden, entwined in ribbons, surrounded by the equally pale animals in the painting "Les Licornes," the unicorns, by Gustave Moreau that hung in his museum in Paris. She could, like the unicorn, "stare the sun out of countenance" with her penetrating azure eyes.

He actually believed, or made himself believe, that God had sent her to him. Yet, he didn't understand why.

Their feelings were obviously mutual, although she always lowered her lids when he spoke to her. She clearly didn't want to see what was in his eyes and didn't want him to see what was in hers. He found himself visiting Glendalough more frequently to visit dear Uncle Diarmid as they had made up after he became a priest. He stayed in his father's house which he had kept and used occasionally for a place to retreat when the bureaucracy and the politics of the Church became too much. It was a small village. He would see her often. One day he asked her if she had been up to the lakes. She had not. He told her it was the most magical place on God's earth. He offered to take her up there for a walk. He stunned himself with his brazenness. It was totally inappropriate. He was equally stunned by her acceptance. Even now, he couldn't believe it happened.

He met her the next morning at eleven. Though it was the beginning of May the weather was unseasonably warm. He was carrying a backpack with a picnic in it. She looked uneasy when she saw the loaf of bread sticking out but said nothing. He had warned her to wear walking shoes and she had on black sneakers which matched her habit. Her headdress was firmly in place. He was wearing his cassock and collar. He thought they looked very chaste. A priest and a nun out for a stroll on a beautiful spring day. But all he could think of were his university days when May 1 rolled around and they all went rollicking in the streets brandishing pints of Guinness chanting, "Hooray, Hooray, the first of May. Outdoor fucking starts today."

There was a true innocence about her, Deirdre, a spiritual innocence, which made him feel guilty and a bit shameful for actually having lustful thoughts. They climbed up to the lakes, pausing briefly to admire their surroundings. The trees were beginning to open their buds and the nascent green had begun to banish the dreary pall of late winter. The river gurgled beside them as they made their way to the top from where it seemed they could see all of Ireland.

It was a glorious day and Fitz was overwhelmed with gladness. He and Deirdre hadn't spoken much along the walk. It was steep in places and he found himself sweating but she was bounding over the rocks and up the path like a gazelle, nary a drop of perspiration on her brow. He was impressed. She was exuberant once they had reached the top and began twirling around the small meadow, her black habit billowing. She began trilling an old Irish ballad. "The Rose of Tralee." It was a song he had sung with his band in another life. She had a high sweet voice and they complimented each other. He wished he had brought his guitar. He was enchanted. It was at that moment he fell hopelessly in love with Dierdre O'Donnell.

Fitz had Father Joseph's attention with his story of Deirdre. He noticed Father Joseph smiling and humming the lyrics of "The Rose of Tralee." Fitz loved those lyrics: "Though lovely and fair as the rose of the summer. Yet 'twas not her beauty alone that won me, Oh no! 'twas the truth in her eye ever dawning that made me love Dierdre . . ."

He listened, relieved to have a break from talking. He couldn't bear to tell Father Joseph what had happened next, but he understood he needed to.

He and Deirdre had decided to walk down the path and have their picnic on the river's edge near his favorite stone. It was where Fitz used to sit as a boy and daydream about what it would be like to have loving parents. The stone was his mate. It had a huge crack in the middle which looked like a smile. Above that were two patches of gray green lichen where its eyes were and on top a thick patch of reddish moss for hair. Fitz named the stone Oisin—or Awsheen—which means "little deer." All his life he had felt like a little deer alone in the forest, but with Awsheen he never had that feeling. Awsheen was always there for him to pour his heart out to. Besides, the real Oisin was a poet and warrior, the son of the great Fionn mac Cumhaill—Finn McCool—his hero. Maybe Fitz thought he could absorb some of the bravery of the McCools by spending time with Awsheen. Deirdre and Fitz picked their spot between Awsheen and an old tree which had fallen into the river, its roots exposed in a twisted display of gnarled gray branches. Fitz unpacked the lunch. A loaf of bread, some sliced ham, cheeses, fruit, and of course, his favorite, chocolate chip cookies. He was so proud of himself for remembering an old blue and white checkered cloth of his mother's and some napkins. Dierdre squealed with pleasure at his little offering and began arranging it around the stump of the tree, a decidedly domestic air about her. With trepidation he pulled out two pints of Guinness and casually put them down on the cloth without looking at her.

"That was bold of you," Father Joseph said, interrupting.

"I thought so," Fitz said.

"What did she do?"

"She said it was lovely. She asked me to open it for her."

"She did?"

"She did. Much to my astonishment. I opened hers and mine and then we clinked bottles in unison. And she chugged it!"

"The fair unicorn maiden?"

"Aye!"

"Keep going. I want to hear more."

Fitz had shaken off his despair and was now animated,

remembering the jolly afternoon he and Dierdre had had together, relishing every detail he could recall for Father Joseph.

"I wanted to know everything about her," Fitz said. "She was obviously unused to talking about herself, a little shy at first but when she got going, she really unwound. She was from Glandore, a beautiful little fishing village in County Cork. Cuan Dor—Harbour of the Oaks. It's a very picturesque town, one of the earliest settlements in Ireland. She was one of eleven children. Her mother was a schoolteacher and her father owned one of the nicest little pubs in town. She worked as a bartender before she decided to become a nun. She knows her ales. Her whiskey, too."

"What compelled her to take her vows?"

"She'd lost a group of friends in a sailing accident. She was the only one to survive. And she was from a very religious family. She had always been devout. She loved Jesus, she prayed to him and the Virgin Mary constantly, carrying around her rosary at all times. She was never really interested in boys, although according to her da, he had to shoo them away with a broom." Fitz met Father Joseph's gaze. "I've become quite close to her kin."

Fitz got up out of his chair and began to walk around the room again. He felt sore from his run. Stiff. He stood for a while looking out the window and stretching. He was craving a Guinness.

"Would you like some water?" Father Joseph seemed to be reading his mind. He didn't wait for an answer but got up and fetched a bottle from the shelf near his chair and handed it to Fitz. Fitz accepted it gratefully.

"Just like Dierdre," he said, tipping his bottle to Father Joseph. "Cheers!"

He took his seat and said, "We talked all afternoon until it was nearly dusk. She was a joyous creature, so merry and full of fun. She laughed a lot and tilted her head a certain way when she looked at me and smiled. I'd spent enough time around women to know what flirting looks like. She was flirting with me. I was not impervious. At one point she tossed off her headdress and her golden curls came tumbling around her shoulders. She told me she was going to wade into the water. She didn't ask this time if I minded. She took off her sneakers. I was blindsided by the eroticism of her gesture."

Fitz was surprised by how comfortable he felt relaying all this intimacy to Father Joseph. There was nothing judgmental about him. Nothing Fitz felt he couldn't say.

He described the way Deirdre walked down to the water's edge toward a strip of marshes which bridged the river from the land, how she lifted up the skirts of her habit and stepped slowly into the moving water, how she let out a little shriek, wobbling as her feet met the muddy bottom. He had known it got deeper on the other side and tried to warn her not to go any further. She had said she was a strong swimmer and plunged through the marsh grasses until she was in the river up to her neck.

"Is this where the story turns?" Father Joseph asked.

"I leapt into the water," Fitz said. "I waded to the marsh grasses, feet dragging me down as I got deeper. Deirdre was struggling, clearly as unused to swimming in her habit as I was in my cassock. I dove in beside her and grabbed her by the waist, pulling her to me as she gasped for breath. She apologized over and over again. I started swimming as hard as I could against the current, finally managing to reach the marsh grasses where the water was shallow. We were able to stand up then, and I tugged at her arms to try to gain some footing for both of us who were mired in the sludge. At last, we made it back to the riverbank and I helped her up to the cloth where she collapsed in exhaustion and, rightly so, protestations of shame and embarrassment.

"It sounds like a mess," Father Joseph said, laughing

"That's what I told her," Fitz said. "I think I said, with the sternest inflection I could muster, 'That was a bloody mess, actually.' But she didn't flinch." Father Joseph chuckled again. "She'd heard it and worse a million times in the pub. And she couldn't very well disagree. She looked so remorseful I could hardly bring myself to remonstrate her. The fact is, she was so beguilingly apologetic that all I wanted to do was scoop her up in my arms." Father Joseph raised one eyebrow. "We decided I would pack up, head down to my car and bring it around as close as I could to the entrance of the path. She would scurry down a discreet distance from me, hide in the bushes and jump into the car when nobody was looking. That was as far as we got."

"How do you mean, 'that was as far as you got?'" asked Father Joseph.

"I didn't intend that as a double entendre," said Fitz, amused. "I had no choice but to take her back to my house and put her things in the dryer once we had rinsed off the mud. Once she had showered, I gave her a white Irish sweater which my mother had knitted and a pair of pants which she rolled up. I showered as well and changed into a black wool turtleneck and black trousers. I felt it only proper to keep the religious colors intact. I gave her a glass of Jameson and poured one for myself. I lit a fire as it had turned chilly. I couldn't help but think that in the movie, this is where they would end up in bed."

Father Joseph threw his head back and roared with laughter.

Fitz laughed too. He was beginning to enjoy this session. It was such a relief to get it out, especially because Father Joseph had not been in the slightest judgmental. But that could change.

After all, he hadn't finished his story. Father Joseph glanced at his watch.

"It's lunch time," he said. "Do you want to continue afterward?"

Fitz hadn't realized how hungry he was. Deep emotion always spurred his appetite.

"Can we meet again?" Fitz asked.

"How's 1:15?" Father Joseph asked, standing slowly.

***

As soon as Deirdre's clothes were dry, Fitz took her home. She was living in a house with several other nuns who were doing charity work near Glendalough. He dropped her off a half mile or so from there so as not to raise any suspicions. She would tell them that she got a ride from a nice couple heading back to Dublin. Another lie. It wasn't that hard.

For the rest of that month, he made his way to Glendalough every weekend. He and Dierdre would always meet at the rock where he had introduced her to Awsheen. No more swimming, even on the hottest of summer days! They talked and talked and talked. They never ran out of things to say. They laughed and laughed. They had picnics. Sometimes she would fix them. She always, always brought chocolate chip cookies. They drank Guinness. She loved Awsheen but she had become particularly attached to the fallen old tree with its exposed tangled roots. "I need a friend too," she said. She pointed to the birds' nest in the top of the tree and remarked that it was shaped like a heart. She named the tree after Awsheen's father, Finn O'Tool, the most legendary warrior in Ireland. Fitz didn't like that. He saw the tree as pathetic and old and weak, not at all the hero he extolled. She saw it as noble and gallant and strong to have survived so much. He couldn't stand to look at it. The crippled tree made him uneasy. Dierdre, on the other hand, cherished the tree. She caressed its mangled roots with her soft white hands as if it were her dying lover. A shrink might have said that Fitz was threatened by Finn. That he was projecting his terror of accepting his own vulnerabilities, whereas she was praising Finn's. She told him she prayed for Finn. She said she prayed for him too. He was never quite sure what she prayed for him about. Perhaps Finn had inspired a premonition in her and in him as well. He sensed nothing but foreboding when she looked at him.

It was everything he could do not to touch her, not to ravage her. She had invited him to with her eyes, but only her eyes. Desire is not an adequate word to describe how he felt about her. The effect she had on him was seismic. He sweated and trembled and stuttered when he was around her. Clearly she had the same feelings for him as he did for her. She also knew, as women are wont to, that she had tremendous power over him, especially when she called him Father and lowered her eyelids and bit her lip. They also understood that what they both wanted was totally unthinkable.

Fitz hadn't seen Sybilla at lunch. He looked for her, even waiting a couple minutes after the others had left, hoping she would show up.

He felt agitated. She had stirred so many emotions in him the night before that he was reeling.

He returned to Father Joseph's office, uncomfortably full. He'd stuffed himself with noodle salad. Father Joseph was sitting, staring out the window.

"Where were we?" Fitz asked, taking his seat.

"What you wanted was unthinkable," Father Joseph said.

Fitz nodded and sat. "Right," he said. "I was about to go on vacation. Normally, I would count the minutes until that time every year, which was the happiest period in my life. But now, as I was about to leave for June on Spetses, I was torn at the thought of leaving her."

Father Joseph sat up in his chair, startled.

"Spetses?" he said.

"Yes, do you know it?" Fitz asked. "It's a Greek island most people have never heard of, and I want to keep it that way."

"I, well no," Father Joseph said. "I don't really, I mean I have heard of it."

"It's paradise," said Fitz. "The most magical place I've ever been.

"While I was in Spetses I thought about nothing but Dierdre. I was in a state of confusion. I could barely function. Finally, I decided that it had to end. I couldn't go on seeing her this way. I had nothing to offer her, nothing to give her. It wasn't fair to her. I was not going to give up the Church. I couldn't. And I would not be one of those hypocritical priests, and believe me there are plenty of them, who are getting a little something on the side, even having babies, and still preen around in their vestments like the vicars of Christ they are not. If I did keep seeing her, I knew that I would lose control and that it would end up destroying both of our lives. I was the man, I was the older one, by a day. I was the priest. I had to do the right thing. I had decided to tell her at the beginning of July when we met at the river. I hadn't seen her for a month. I hadn't contacted her at all. She arrived after I did. I was leaning up against Awsheen, waiting for her to come, gazing out at the river, happy to be back in Ireland but still in my Spetses daze. I was quivering with giddy anticipation and at the same time profound sorrow at the prospect of seeing her again, knowing it would be the last time."

"And was it?"

"She came hurrying up the hill, breathless, her headdress askew as usual, her face flushed with pleasure and excitement, an expectant smile on her lips. She looked radiantly beautiful. My heart plunged to the bottom of my stomach. She came at me and before I knew what was happening, she threw her arms around me and held me as tightly as she could. She told me she had missed me terribly. She begged me to say that I had missed her too. I couldn't stop holding her. I felt deeply that she belonged in my arms. It was the most natural thing in the world. We were meant to be together. Why would God have sent her to me? Or sent me to her? I felt as if I would lose my balance. I was besotted. I couldn't begin to let her go. We rocked back and forth in each other's embrace for a long while. Then she raised her head and looked up at me, into my eyes, held her mouth up to mine. I could feel her breath. There was a fleeting moment when I hesitated, but it was no use. I brushed her lips softly, tentatively. I wanted to make sure this what she really wanted. It was what she really wanted. She brushed mine. I couldn't take it anymore. I crushed her mouth in mine, and she responded. I would have had her right then and there, but it was too risky. I told her I was going to get the car and that she should meet me at the bottom of the hill. We drove in silence back to my house. She placed her hand on my thigh. I nearly wrecked the car. I in my cassock, she in her habit. A priest and a nun. Who would have thought they were about to fuck their brains out." Father Joseph laughed. "Hooked, are ye?" Fitz asked.

"You might say. You're a good storyteller. Besides, it's gratifying to see people like you struggle with their consciences. It makes me feel less guilty."

"I think I can best you there."

Father Joseph waited expectantly.

"I don't need to tell you what happened."

"Oh, go ahead."

They both laughed.

"We barely made it into the house," Fitz said. "All I can tell you is that, God forgive me, it was the first time I have ever really experienced the Divine. I loved God, I loved Jesus, I loved the Virgin Mary. But never like this. We made love. We loved each other. Not just our bodies entwined but our souls as well. I could only think that God had created us for this purpose. It was his doing. It was transcendent. I had never been in love before. I hadn't even understood the concept. Now everything became clear to me. I didn't feel guilt or shame at all. I didn't feel I had sinned. I felt as if I were doing God's will. So did Dierdre. We both cried a lot. The tears were mixed. Joy and sorrow, loneliness and longing. We shed tears of gratitude that the Lord had brought us to this moment. We made our own vows to each other. To love one another for as long as we shall live. And yes, we were aware we had made the same vows to the Church. You can debate who we made our vows to. Some would say God. But the Church doesn't always represent God. The Church, in our minds, was suddenly an institution. The Church was not made in God's image. We were. And we were together because of him."

"You sound pretty sure of that."

"I am. Or rather I was."

"Was?"

"I keep going back to that line of your mate, Thomas Merton. 'Love is our true destiny. We do not find the meaning of life by ourselves alone. We find it with another.' That other was Dierdre. We were each other's true destiny. We were the meaning of each other's lives. The next two months were a mix of bliss and hell. Before Dierdre and I had really had time to discuss what had happened, she was called back to her convent as it was summer and school was out. We had no real way to communicate. We were unable to even think about making plans, whatever those plans might be. Certainly, we had not discussed leaving the Church although it was obviously on both of our minds. I was dispatched to Rome, ostensibly to study the encyclicals. In fact, as I began to realize, I was being groomed for bigger things. I was distraught on one level, missing her with all of my heart. On the other hand, I was elated at my reception in Rome and the way I was being introduced to the powers that be as though I had a real future. I didn't like that about myself. But there it was."

"What happened with Dierdre?"

Fitz put his arms on the table and buried his head in them, then pulled himself up out of the chair and walked over to the wall, his lanky figure bent over in pain. He pounded his right fist against it, shocking even himself.

"I killed her, Father," he said. "I was as responsible for her death as if I had actually strangled her with my own hands."

Father Joseph stood and approached Fitz. He reached out and gently pulled Fitz's shaking arms down and held them in his.

"Now, dear boy," Father Joseph said in a soothing voice. "You certainly don't look like a killer to me. And I grant you God doesn't think you are one either. Why don't you come over to your chair and sit down."

He led a compliant Fitz back to the table and helped ease him down into his seat. Fitz leaned his head back as far as he could, ran his fingers through his tousled hair and across his drenched face and let out a deep breath.

"Oh God," he said finally. "God in heaven. Help me. Show me the way. I'm so lost." He quickly reached for a tissue to stave off the torrent.

"Tell me what happened," said Father Joseph.

AFTER AGONIZING THE WHOLE TIME that he was in Rome, it finally became clear to Fitz what he had to do. He was going to leave the Church. He was going to turn away from the institution—not from God. He realized he could love God and Deirdre. God has always said that love is infinite, and he thought that he could serve him better by being a loving husband and father than he could as a hypocritical wayward priest.

He could hardly wait to get to Awsheen to see her, to tell her. But he was shocked when he saw her. She arrived looking pale and gaunt. She wasn't her usual self. She didn't laugh. She was uncharacteristically silent. He asked her if she was alright. She said she hadn't been feeling well lately but she was sure it was nothing. He finally got her to confess that she had been having splitting headaches, possibly because her vision was blurry. She was losing weight, most likely because she was vomiting a lot. She had had a seizure. She said she wasn't thinking straight.

He could see that she was speaking haltingly. He asked her if she had seen a doctor. She had not. He didn't wait a second. He started down the hill to the car, shouting at her to follow him. She could barely climb into the car. He decided to drive her to the emergency room at St. Joseph hospital in Dublin. It was only forty-five minutes away and he wanted to make sure she got the best care. A few of his classmates at Trinity College were there. He insisted on going in with her, despite her protestations.

He explained to the admitting doctor that she was a teacher in one of their schools and he had just learned of her illness and was the only one with a car. They agreed to see her right away, very deferential to the two of them. They were obviously good Catholics. That always helped.

She gave him a glance of sheer terror when they put her in a wheelchair and took her away. He spent the rest of the day in the waiting room, occasionally asking after her but not wanting to seem too frantic. Luckily it was Saturday and he was off duty. Unluckily it was Saturday and by the time evening rolled around, every drunk in Dublin was being brought in bleeding from pub fights all over town. He was starving but afraid to go to the cafeteria for fear the doctors would come out to speak with him. Finally, he rushed down to get a cup of hot tea and a sandwich of undetermined contents and some fruit. Just as he got back, the doctors called him in. He went to her cubicle. She was hooked up to everything. She looked at him with a wan smile, then turned her head away. He wanted to hold her, but he knew that wouldn't be appropriate. The doctor looked grim, gave him a moment, and then took him back out to the hallway. "I'm sorry, Father," he said. "I have bad news. The good sister is suffering from late-stage Glioblastoma..." Brain cancer. Incurable. The doctor said he'd like to keep her there for a few days for observation. The doctor asked where she lived. The truth was, he didn't really know. He told the doctor that she had been at a convent and he understood that she lived in a house with other nuns in Glendalough.

"I'll find out more and let you know as soon as I can," he said. He was thinking fast. "Doctor, would you mind if I spend a moment alone with her to pray?"

"Of course not, Father," the doctor said with some reverence. "Please spend as much time as you like."

He went in to see her. She was curled up in a fetal position, facing away from him.

"Macushla, my darling," he said to her.

She didn't respond. He went around to the other side and sat on the edge of the bed facing her. He began stroking her wispy hair. He was trying to control his emotions. A tear slid down her cheek.

"I'm so sorry," she whispered.

"Sorry for what?"

"I wanted to live so that I could love you. You do know that I love you with all of my heart." He didn't know what to say. "You can love me. I'm right here. I will always be here in your heart and you in mine."

She lifted her eyes to look at him.

"Why did God do this to me? To us? I thought he had sent us to be together. I really believed that. Which was why I succumbed." She gave a weak smile. "To your charms." She wiped away her tears. "I think God did. I think it was Jesus. I think Jesus was jealous of our relationship. All of these years I gave myself to him. I think he wanted to be the only one." She started sobbing. "I feel so betrayed. I think I hate Jesus." He lifted her up and held her tightly in his arms. He didn't care if anyone saw them. She buried her face in his neck.

He didn't know whether this was the right time to tell her, but he had to.

"Deirdre," he whispered. "I want to leave the Church. I want to marry you."

She turned away, but he could still feel her tears on his neck.

"You can't leave the Church," she said, choking. "The Church is your home. And I want to go to mine. Please take me home. I don't mean to heaven. I mean to my family. I don't want to die in a hospital or in the convent. I want to die at home. That way you can come see me. We can be together until the end. Please!" Her eyes were beseeching him. He had no choice. He called her family and arranged for her to be taken home. The convent was not happy, but they had no sway over him or her anymore. She wanted to go up to the lake one more time, to sit by Awsheen and fondle her beloved Finn McCool, but it was not to be. Frankly, he was glad. It would have been too painful for him to see her so sick there. He wanted to remember the exuberant figure she had been, not who she now was.

He went to Glandore as often as he could get away to see her. She had lost so much weight that she was barely recognizable. It didn't take long for her to be confused about who he was. She could sense he was somebody she loved, and she wanted him to hold her, but after a few visits she wasn't really there much of the time. She would have seizures and then she would sleep. They never discussed their love for each other again. He would tell her he loved her. What else was there to say? "Don't leave me," was all she could utter. It was then that he placed his mother's Claddagh ring on her finger, the point of the heart facing hers.

Her family was obviously curious about their friendship, but he didn't think they suspected the truth. For them it was unthinkable. They knew he felt a sense of obligation because he had been the one to take her to the hospital. And he was the one who prayed with her, though she didn't want to pray any more. He prayed with them. They took comfort in that. He did not. Nothing comforted him in those days. He had never been so confused in his life.

He was there when she died. It was right before Christmas. December 20. Her birthday and the day after his. The family was surrounding her bed. He told her he was there. He gave her last rites. He wasn't sure she wanted that, but he had no choice with everyone watching. He was holding her hand. He bent down to kiss her forehead and whispered in her ear. "Macushla, I will always love you until the end of time." He believed she heard him. She squeezed his hand. Then she was gone. And with her his heart. Of course he went to her funeral. The service was lovely. The church was decked out with holiday finery. It was a beautiful gusty December day. Afterward, everyone present walked out to the meadow overlooking the sea and scattered red roses into the wind. All he could think of was that first time they took their walk to the lake and she was twirling around atop the mountain singing "The Rose of Tralee."

I slept through breakfast and lunch. When I finally woke after two, I jumped out of bed in a semi stupor, stunned at the hour. Oddly, I had slept the sleep of the dead. I had never been so emotionally wrung out in my life. What had happened with Fitz the night before still hadn't sunk in. In fact, I didn't even really trust my memory. I wasn't sure that it hadn't been a dream.

I quickly threw on a blue sleeveless shift and some walking sandals and raced up the stairs to the dining room, composing myself as I entered and briefly scanned the area. I knew Fitz wouldn't be there, but I looked for him anyway. There was no sign of him.

Hungry, I grabbed a cup of coffee. Dave was passing in the hall and saw me. He came over with a piece of banana bread, an offering of sorts. He had such sad eyes but his smile was hopeful. He nodded as he placed it cautiously in front of me. I didn't have the heart to refuse. I smiled back and accepted the bread. Actually, I was grateful. It saved me from making a decision. A look of gratitude spread over Dave's face, and he let out a sigh as he walked out again. I wondered if he or the others had noticed I hadn't shown up for all of the services or all of the meals.

I headed back to my room to gather my thoughts before the service. I lay on the bed and stared at the ceiling. My mind was blank. This is what is supposed to happen when you meditated. Was I meditating? I thought about what I was feeling. I was feeling nothing. No pain, no joy, no anger, no fear. Nothing. I wasn't sleeping. I wasn't daydreaming. I wasn't fantasizing. The only way I could think of to describe what I was going through was some sort of metamorphosis. I came here confused, not knowing who I was anymore, having lost myself. Something was changing but I didn't quite understand it yet. I wasn't comfortable with it either. But it was there. It was happening and I would just have to go with it. To let it happen.

I could barely drag myself off of the bed at 2:45 to get up the hill to the chapel in time for Lauds. I was sure he would be there. No sight of him. The horrible thought crossed my mind that he might have left. I could certainly see why. What had happened must have undone him. He had to realize, as did I, that it was, on the surface, totally inappropriate. Yet it wasn't. What had happened was a spontaneous act of love, of charity. Who could have known, could have predicted that we would fall in love with each other in those precious few moments we had together? Because that is what happened. I knew now that I had fallen in love with him. There was no doubt in my mind that he had fallen in love with me. He might not have realized it yet but what had affected both of us was so powerful that it couldn't be denied. I could see the dismay in his eyes. So, of course, he would have had to leave. He had no choice. I was bereft. My lurching stomach and dry mouth only exacerbated the sorrow. It was all I could do to sit through the service.

When it was over, I couldn't get down to the river fast enough. I'm not a runner but I simply flew out the chapel doors and down the road. It was hot and the sun was baking down on me. I had forgotten to put on sunblock too. I would look like an old hag soon if I kept forgetting.

Past the outdoor chapel I went turning toward the natural cemetery where I wished I could have stopped and simply expired on the spot. The pain I had not been feeling earlier in my meditative state was suddenly upon me, engulfing my lungs, searing my gut. I got down past the dilapidated barn and followed the path to the river's edge. From there I turned right and tore through the woods, tripping over stones and roots and slipping on dead leaves, almost falling at one point.

At last, I came upon the place I had found the day before. It was a place which sloped down to the water's edge with a few stepping stones out into the river. If I wanted to, I could slip off my sandals and wade rather than be on the steep embankment I had just passed. There was an old tree I could lean against. I needed support. I sat down and tried to catch my breath, sweating profusely. I blotted my forehead with the skirt of my blue shift and settled myself.

My brain was running amok. I tried inhaling and exhaling slowly and deliberately until I achieved a certain rhythm. I looked at the river, serene, tranquil. I envisioned myself as floating on it, peaceful, assured of my destination. Slowly I began to climb out of my despair. I looked up and noticed a long thin switch of bark from a bush almost waving at me. It was full of leaves, peaking in golden hues. I reached out and broke it off. I held it for a while. At once I remembered that today was Rosh Hashanah, the Jewish New Year. We had been invited to a friend's house in Long Island for Tashlich this year, but I was going to be here at the monastery and had to regret. I had always loved the ceremony of throwing something, usually breadcrumbs in the ocean to symbolize the casting away of sins. Not that I thought I had that many sins. Sometimes I would make wishes instead. Probably not kosher but my heart was in the right place. Half consciously I began to pluck the yellow leaves one by one. Sort of "he loves me, he loves me not." As I did so I would throw each leaf into the water at my feet and watch it get carried away. My sin: wanting to break my marriage vows. My wish: breaking my marriage vows. My sin: lusting after a Catholic archbishop. My wish: bedding the Catholic archbishop. My sin: wanting him to break his vows to the Church. My wish: wanting him to break his vows to the Church. My sin: I couldn't think of another one. My wish: X-rated. My sin: the previous wish.

If Fitz was gone, I needed to start again. But how? How did I get to this empty place to begin with? Where? Where to go to find the Sybilla I once was? I liked her. I wanted to be her again.

Maman was a devotee of all things supernatural. She had inculcated in me the belief that there was something bigger than we were and, like the good Catholic she was, it didn't necessarily have to be God.

Of course, there was always God, but the occult was just another way to reach God more rapidly and, I have to admit, more entertaining. Maman was also very superstitious, when I had my confirmation in our little private chapel in Spetses she had given me a thin gold chain necklace with tiny evil eyes on it and instructed me never to take it off. I never had. Maman has a fabulous French astrologer in Paris, Didier, an elegant, beautifully mannered, highly educated older gentleman she had introduced me to on my eighteenth birthday.

When Spraig and I were thinking of getting married I immediately called Didier. He was not at all sanguine. He pointed out that Spraig was a Leo with a tendency toward narcissism and that I should be careful. I didn't want to hear it and wouldn't speak to Didier for at least a year after that. Sometimes now I wish I had listened to him but then I'm not sure I would have changed anything. We did have a wonderful time together in those first years. I had consulted Didier again when we found out Spraig was infertile. He told me Saturn was in my sign and would be for several years. That is also not good. Saturn is a bear. Saturn in your sign is the school of hard knocks. One does get through it which is fine if you're still standing. I was, but only with an emotional walker.

Fitz, I had just learned on Google, was a Sagittarius. I'm a double Cancer. Cancer and Sagittarius was the worst combination in the zodiac, totally incompatible. Cancers loved being at home. All Sagittarius wanted to do was fly away. And that he had clearly done.

Maman and I also flirted with psychics, tarot card readers, mediums, and palmists. Some were amazing, others, complete charlatans. Father and Spraig thought only idiots trafficked in this stuff. Spraig knew about Didier specifically. He was contemptuous of him. If only he knew what Didier had said about him. The funny thing was, whenever I told him I had an appointment with Didier he couldn't wait to ask what he'd said. It was all I could do not to laugh in his face. I never told him the whole truth. I usually said something innocuous like he was very ambitious and would be successful in his career. That satisfied him and had the benefit of being true.

Maman and I also had a secret fortuneteller we would never have told Father or Spraig about. He was a French speaking Moroccan shaman named Mustapha. Mustapha lived outside of Marrakesh in a mountain village and claimed that presidents, first ladies, queens, emirs, sultans, etc. had come to visit him in their limousines with their entourages. Maman found him through a French diplomat who had been posted in Morocco. He came highly recommended. The thing is, Mustapha was almost always right. Sometimes his predictions were realized immediately. Other times they didn't come to fruition until several years later. But he had never been wrong. Which was why we kept going back to him and paying him way more than we should. The problem was that Mustapha was a pain in the ass. He always needed money. He wanted it wired immediately or he would lose his house, he wouldn't be able to pay for his family medical expenses, they would starve. He also needed money for "matériels," for his deliberations, like candles and incense. Even when he contacted Maman and me to say that there was a Moroccan feast and he couldn't afford the mutton for his family dinner, Maman sent him some money. However, and this is a big however, the last time I spoke to him this past summer he told me another man was going to come into my life unexpectedly and that it would be very serious for both of us. I was so low that I dismissed his prognostication out of hand. Now I was thinking maybe I should send him some money for his mutton.

Although it was probably over. Fitz had left.

The sun was casting shadows on the other side of the river.

Why then, did I feel a subtle change in my demeanor? What part of this soul-searching had delivered to me some insight, some clarity? I had to find myself before I could find anyone else, even Fitz. As cliched as it was, I had to put the oxygen mask over my mouth before his.

I was hot. The very last of the breeze had died down and the air was still. The water was lapping up against the shore, just begging me to come in. I thought I might wade a bit. I stepped out of my sandals and walked gingerly across the small stones, submerging my feet as I went. It felt so delicious and had a cooling effect on my whole body. On a sudden impulse, I tore off my shift, stripping down to my pale blue matching bra and panties, waded in hip deep and plunged. Nothing had ever felt so good. The water was soft, moving gently and not terribly deep. The marsh grasses were growing on the other side. I submerged myself, letting the river embrace me. It was murmuring in my ears, as if trying to send me a message. I started to float letting it carry me slowly downstream. It struck me that this was a baptism of sorts. Not that I needed to be relieved of my sins. I had done that already. It was more that I needed to be cleansed of all the old wounds. I needed my sorrows to be washed away. I needed to be saved. I needed to be, for lack of a better phrase, born again. At once I felt totally at peace.

Then, without warning, I felt a sharp pain in my thigh. I doubled over in surprise. It gripped my leg and came over me in waves. My leg was cramping, something I hadn't experienced in years. It was debilitating. I cried out. It didn't stop. It had moved down to my calf and then to my foot, which was twisted, inversely. I couldn't move, couldn't begin to swim or even paddle my way to shore with my arms. I yelled again and shut my eyes in agony. There was nothing I could do. I was helpless.

I don't know where he came from. All I know is that he had both of his arms under mine and he was dragging me back to shore.

He began to pull me out of the water, but I shrieked, "Cramp, cramp!" and began pointing to my leg. I was struggling with him and he was having a difficult time calming me down. Finally, he dragged me to the edge of the river, so I was half in half out. He shifted me again until I was fully on the ground and then began to stretch me and massage my thigh. All I could do was moan and bend toward my leg. Before I knew it, he had me on my feet, hoisting me with one of my arms around his neck and forcing my leg down, still rubbing, forcing me to put my weight on it. "Uh, uh, uh," was all the noise I could make.

We stood together, he keeping pressure on me until gradually the spasms subsided and I could breathe.

"Okay, okay," I said. He helped me down to a sitting position so that I could lean against a giant stone. Near the stone was a fallen tree, its roots exposed in a giant tangled, gnarled mess. I sat there for a few minutes, catching my breath in silence, my eyes closed. When I finally opened them, Fitz was sitting opposite me, his eyes held a mixture of concern and amusement. He couldn't conceal the sweeping glance he gave my body. I would like to imagine it was approving. At first, I was stunned. He was here! He hadn't left! I tried very hard not to show my elation, although the electricity between us was hard to ignore.

I was no longer in pain but until that moment I hadn't focused on the fact that I was not entirely clothed. I looked down, gave out a little yelp and quickly placed one hand over my breasts and the other over my crotch to limit my exposure. He burst out laughing.

"Oh my God," I said, horribly embarrassed.

He put his finger over his lips and made a shushing noise.

It was, after all, a silent retreat.

Okay, I thought. *If that's how you want it, I can play that game too.* I nodded. My underwear was completely soaked. So were his clothes. His black t-shirt clung to his chest and his black jeans were totally waterlogged, as were his sneakers. I noticed he was wearing a St. Christopher's medal, the medal to protect travelers on their journeys, to bring health, prosperity, and faith. He is also the patron saint of strength. He was said to be tall and strong and well-built. How apt!

The tension was palpable. I didn't know what to do. I'd never felt so self-conscious. He didn't make a move. He just kept looking at me. I was riveted by his sloping eyebrows, at once empathetic, quizzical, and seductive. Then, almost reluctantly, he gazed out at the river. I couldn't stand it anymore. I slowly got up, testing my leg, which was fine by now and pointed to where my clothes were up the path a bit. I started to walk but the pebbles under my feet were jagged. Sensing my discomfort, he jumped up and took my arm. I found my spot on the edge of the river where my shift and sandals were. I quickly pulled the dress over my head to cover myself.

Naturally, wet spots appeared from the waterlogged bra and panties. I may as well not have bothered. I looked around for my switch, the one I had relieved of its leaves. It was there near the water, lying crooked between the little river stones. I walked over to pick it up and then turned back to him. He beckoned me to sit down. I did without even hesitating, without even questioning. I leaned against the tree. He reached down and pulled off his t-shirt and began to wring it out. Jesus! I stifled a surprised gasp as I looked at his slim, muscled torso, his chest revealing curly black hair with only a few wisps of gray. He seemed totally oblivious to the effect he was having on me. He hung his shirt over a branch and sat down next to me. I couldn't imagine what he was going to do next. I knew what I wanted him to do but that was never going to happen. He turned to me, reached over, and took the switch out of my hand. A sudden humorous thought flashed across my mind. Don't tell me His Grace was into S and M and was going to flay me? A shiver of anticipation ran through my warped brain. I couldn't suppress a smile. He smiled back. We held each other's gaze for what seemed like an eternity. If Shakespeare was right and "the eyes are the window to your soul," I saw through his as clearly as I had ever seen anything. I saw the pain and longing and love and loneliness and fear and regret and shame. I saw the decency and the intelligence and the humor and the dedication and the passion and the honor and the sense of duty. At that moment I really knew him and the more I knew him the more I really loved him.

Before I could figure out what he was going to do with the switch, he gently began to trace my profile with the bare point of it. He touched the top of my head, brushing a lock of my hair behind my ear. He ran the switch down the slope of my nose. He touched my cheeks. He stroked my lips, first the top lip and then the bottom lip, carefully, precisely. He dwelt on my mouth until I was mesmerized. He never took his eyes away from mine. He ran the switch around my chin and down to my neck. He moved it around my neck, first to the right side under my ear and then to the left. I shivered. Down he went to the V-neck in my shift, touching my chest ever so softly. He swirled the switch around my breasts barely touching them. He moved to my arms, first one then the other. He started under the arm of my sleeveless dress tickling me just enough and then moved on down the rest of my arm to the inside of my wrists, then between my fingers. At this point I was about to faint. He came back to my stomach. I could feel a wrench in my groin. Without any hesitation he slid the branch down to the V between my legs. He didn't linger but kept going, taking first one thigh, then the other. My shift was above my knees and my legs were exposed. He placed the switch behind my knee, then swirled it around my calf. He did the same with the other leg. I was immobilized. He came to my feet, tracing them each, first the tops, then the soles, then in between each of my toes. I had never really understood the meaning of the word swoon before. Now I did.

We were still looking into each other's eyes. When he was finished, he didn't hesitate. He brought the switch to his mouth and kissed it.

He stood up, reached for my hand, and pulled me up as well. I wondered then if he would kiss me, but he made no move to do so. He handed me back my switch. He gestured for me to go. I looked at him one last time, put on my sandals, turned away from him, and practically staggered up the slope to the road. It was beginning to get dark and much cooler. There was no way either of us was going to make the five-thirty Vespers.

I sneaked into the guest house, making sure nobody was about and ran down the stairs to my room. I couldn't wait to get into the shower and allow myself the luxury of letting the hot water run over my hair and my face and my body. The body he had just claimed.

I lay on the bed for a while, trying to make sense of the intensity of what had just happened. I thought Fitz was the most charismatic person I had ever met. I had thought so when I had seen him on TV, but he was much more so in person. I had always known that charisma was about charm, power, and inspiration. But his charisma was different. His was a spiritual gift of grace, of love, divined from God. I could feel it. So could others.

Was this a fantasy? Was I going to have an affair with the Archbishop of Dublin? There's an old saying I always thought was corny but it seemed apt for this moment. "When someone told me I lived in a fantasyland I nearly fell off my unicorn." I guess I should saddle up.

I was going to dinner. I wondered if he would be there. Just in case, I curled my hair, put on my jeans and some ballet slippers and a loose fitting, wide neck, light blue cashmere sweater. I certainly didn't need any blusher. My face was already in a postcoital flush. Just the slightest amount of eye shadow, a tiny bit of mascara, a dash of pale lipstick and I was ready.

There was the dinner bell. I'd had a huge lunch but was still starving.

I went up to the dining room. The whole gang was there. He was not. I tried to hide my disappointment. Was he really going to disappear on me again? I poured a glass of water and took it to my place, then got a plate and served myself. White chicken chili, corn bread, and cottage cheese. Not bad.

Dave gave me a shy smile. Oh dear. I tried not to make eye contact with the others but I had missed Vespers and so had Fitz. I hoped nobody was getting suspicious. I noticed the ladies were more dolled up than usual. I doubted it was for Dave or Krish. Just when I began to despair, in came Fitz. He owned the room. You could hear them clank when he walked, as Father used to say. He seemed even more imposing tonight. He exuded confidence.

Was I imagining it or was there a joyousness about him which I had not seen? The sadness which had hovered over him had disappeared. He was totally different. His joy became mine. He didn't look at me. I think it would have been curtains if we had so much as exchanged a glance. The others, particularly Arianthe and Deedee, were clearly fascinated by the two of us, not knowing anything of course. But then again lust was simply oozing out of our every pore.

He got his plate, wolfed down his dinner, had seconds, and then got some pie for dessert. I wasn't having any dessert, but I didn't want to leave his presence. I had to leave, though. It would be odd for me to just sit there, not eating. I went back to my room to wait for Compline at seven-thirty. Maybe that would settle my nerves.

I put on a light jacket and left my room early, not looking at his door. I got my flashlight and went up to the chapel. I was the first one there. I took my usual place at the back on the aisle next to the door. I was feeling excited and anxious at the same time. I didn't want to turn my head to look at the door, so when the bells sounded, I had to force myself to stare straight ahead.

The others drifted in one by one and took their places. Fitz was the last to arrive. He walked up to the front, bowed to the cross, sat in his usual spot at the end of the second row, crossed himself, and knelt.

Curiosity nearly killed me. What was he praying about? Was he asking forgiveness for his sins? For his obvious display of lust toward me? For the fact that his love of God and Christ may not be as strong as it should be? Was he promising to pay a penance? Ghost me? Leave? Never see me again? That I couldn't bear. Or was he thanking God for bringing me into his life? For allowing him to love again, to desire again. My guess was none of the above. He was praying to God to help him find his way, guide him do the right thing, allow him to make an honorable decision. It was the most sacred of petitionary prayers.

The darkness of the room, the chanting of the monks, the flickering of the candles all served to soothe me. I was not praying. I was not even meditating. I was waiting. Waiting to see what he would do next. In a way I felt helpless. Despite what had transpired this afternoon, it was still up to him to make the next move. We had both taken vows. If we broke those vows the consequences for me would be minor. For him, they would be devastating.

I couldn't in good conscience lead him into something he would regret later. I didn't want the responsibility for that. He had to take responsibility for his own actions. I could wait. I should wait. I had to wait. I had no other choice.

I took off immediately as the service was ending, before the last monk had departed, and raced down the hill. I didn't want another awkward flashlight incident. Besides, I had mine firmly in hand. Once I was in my room, I flopped down on the bed and . . . waited. I could feel that something would happen. All of that pent up sexual energy had to go somewhere. I just didn't know where.

I don't know how long it was before I heard a slight scratching noise. I jumped up and ran over to see what it was. A letter had been slipped under my door. It was a large, handsome ecru envelope. It was addressed to Ms. Sybilla Sumner. I grabbed it and ran to my bed to read it. In the upper left-hand corner was engraved in green ink, "The Archbishop of Dublin." I tore it open. The thick paper had the same thing engraved in green at the top.

In bold script it read:

"The Archbishop of Dublin requests the pleasure of the company of Ms. Sybilla Sumner for a shot of Jameson whiskey. Nine p.m. Room 7. Informal." It's a good thing I was lying down or I would have passed out. It was almost eight-thirty. He thoughtfully gave me time to "freshen up." I went to the bathroom mirror to survey the damage. I brushed my teeth and squirted breath spray in my mouth. My hair definitely needed work. I had taken a shower earlier but had not curled it. Out came the electric rollers. I didn't want to put on too much makeup. I was going for the natural look. That meant very sheer foundation, light eyeliner, the tiniest bit of mascara, pale blusher over my whole face, soft pink lipstick which I put on and then wiped off (just in case) and a touch of lip gloss. The rollers had given me enough body without looking like I had spent the day at the salon. No hairspray. I decided to keep on the blue sweater I was wearing. It would look like I was trying too hard if I changed. Finally, I dabbed my neck, (crucial) and in between my breasts and my wrists with Sortilege. I was definitely going to need sorcery tonight. It was nine p.m. As I was about to leave, I glanced down at the gold band on my left hand. My wedding ring, engraved with fleurs-de-lis. On the inside was, "You are the light of my life. S.S. and S.E." It was Spraig's concession to me.

For a second I thought about taking it off, then decided against it. Not yet. I took one last look in the mirror, pronounced myself presentable, drew in my breath, let it out, and headed across the hall to his room. I paused before I knocked.

My hands were shaking so I held them together in front of me. I decided praying would be inappropriate. Dear God, please let me get laid? I didn't think so.

Happily, he opened the door quickly, as I was worried about being seen. He looked so tall. His thick curly hair was slightly tousled. I hadn't really noticed before, but he clearly hadn't shaved since he'd been here and there was a two-day growth on his chin. He was wearing a black, long-sleeved pullover and black jeans, which he had worn at dinner. His Saint Christopher's medal was hanging outside of his shirt. He smiled and nodded toward the room, beckoning me inside. He closed the door behind me. I noticed that he had taken the desk chair from one side of the room and moved it over to the other side next to the armchair. There would be no sitting on the bed. At first, anyway. He had left only one light on, the lamp on the desk. The floor lamp behind the armchair and the one on the bedside table were off. He motioned me to sit in the armchair. On the desk was a bottle of Jameson. Next to it was one silver engraved cup. Next to that was a piece of his stationary, on which he had written a few notes. He walked over, picked it up, handed it to me, then went back to the desk and poured some whiskey into the cup.

I began to read.

"Carl Jung on the Unicorn Cup," it read. "It is called the Healing Cup. Cardinal Juan de Torquemada (the good Torquemada) always kept one on his table. It is said: '*La Corne de licorne preserves les sortileges.*' (The horn of the unicorn preserves sorcery.)" He turned to me, came over, took a seat in the other chair, and handed the cup to me.

It was made of thick, heavy silver, obviously an antique. On it was an exquisite unicorn carved in bas relief. It was only about three inches in height. It fit perfectly in my hand. I gasped in delight and ran my finger slowly over the carving, feeling its strength. I looked at him for permission, lifting the glass to my lips. He nodded again and I drank.

The burning sensation was exceeded only by the sensation I had between my legs. I took a gulp this time and nearly choked. It was smooth though, and it felt delicious sliding down the back of my throat and into my stomach. I could feel my body start to tingle and burn. He laughed and reached over to me with an imploring gesture. I was a bit chagrined at having failed to offer him the second drink. I grinned sheepishly and handed him the cup. I had the distinct feeling he might have had a wee taste before I got there. He took one long swig, cocked his head at me, and then took another. He looked down at the empty cup, went over to the desk for a refill and then sat back down. It was my turn. I took two very long shots. It was going to my head quite quickly, but I had to say I felt very relaxed, almost giddy. I started to laugh out loud, an excited deep-throated laugh which came from down in my gut. I hadn't laughed like that in years. He followed suit with two more shots and started bellowing with laughter, his even deeper than mine. Back he went for a refill, two more for me, two more for him until we were holding our sides with mirth, tears running down our cheeks, gasping for air, both of us caught up in the absurdity of the situation, the insanity of what we were doing, incredulous at the enormous risk we were taking.

The relief was extraordinary. All of the pent-up anger and fear and hurt we were both carrying came bursting out of our lungs until we were both about to explode. Fitz reached in his pocket and handed me a handkerchief, then got another from the bedside table drawer for himself. We had quieted down by now, wiping our faces and taking deep breaths and sighing at the same time. Once the emotions had subsided, we sat very still, totally silent looking into each other's eyes. I went limp, unable to divert my gaze.

Before I knew what was happening, he stood up, reached down, took both of my hands in his and pulled me up to him. Never taking his eyes away, he cupped my chin in both of his hands. He began to kiss the top of my head as he caressed my hair. He kissed my forehead. He kissed my ears, he kissed my neck, hovering gently, his soft breath sending a tingling sensation up and down my spine. I held my face up to him to receive his lips. He didn't kiss them. Instead, he pulled each one of my hands to his mouth and, caressing them, began to run his lips over my outstretched palms. First the insides, then the back of my hands, followed by my fingers. He kept my hands in his as he pushed me away, held me apart from him and looked at me hungrily. I realized what he was doing. He wanted me to come to him. He wouldn't have it any other way. He needed to know that I wanted him as badly as he wanted me. I very carefully stepped toward him. I wanted to make a declaration with my movements. I put my arms around his neck and clasped my hands. I pulled myself to his chest and, with deliberation, I began to lightly brush his lips with mine. A slight brush and then I pulled away. Another slight brush and I pulled away again. He put his arms around my waist but let me take the lead. This time I parted my lips and did it again. He did the same. Now we were touching each other's open mouths, but I kept pulling away after each encounter.

The sexual tension was excruciating. I didn't know how much longer I could go on but before I had the chance to pull away again, he tightened his arms around my waist and pressed his mouth to mine, nearly devouring me with his lips, his tongue, his teeth. His hands were all over me, up my back and my neck and in my hair, on my breasts, down my back again and on my derriere, just grazing between my legs. We were biting each other, not just our lips but our necks and shoulders, sucking on each other, almost in desperation. We were both panting and groaning with longing, with need. He picked me up and carried me to the bed, laying me down. This time he was not so gentle. He took my shoes off, flung them on the floor and then unzipped my jeans and had them off within seconds. He pulled my sweater over my head and that went on the floor as well. He stood back appraising me with satisfaction in my lace bra and panties. I didn't even have to help him take them off. He unhooked my bra one handed with such expertise it was stunning.

I spread my arms above my head and my legs wide on the bed, waiting to be taken. He kicked his shoes off and tore off his T-shirt. That gorgeous, muscular chest again. He began to unzip his jeans. He wore black stretch boxer briefs, the large bulge which I had felt when he was kissing me now painfully evident. He pulled down his briefs and stepped out of them, unconsciously grabbing and needlessly stroking himself. He surveyed me again, this time it would seem, planning his attack. He didn't just throw himself on top of me. He stepped to the foot of the bed, got on his knees, and began to creep until he was completely over me but not touching me. He swayed back and forth several times in a rhythmic motion. I could feel part of him between my legs, just brushing me the way I had done to him with my lips. I had to swallow hard to contain myself. The desire in my breasts, in the pit of my stomach, in my groin was overwhelming. I realized again that he was going to wait for me to come to him. I arched my back to meet him. That was all he needed.

Suddenly his body met mine and completely overtook me. From then on it was almost a blur of such intense yearning that I can barely remember. He kissed me deeply, and I kissed him back. He moved back down to my feet and began kissing and licking his way up. When he got to where he wanted, he buried his head in me. He knew exactly what to do with his tongue, where to put it, what to caress, what would excite me the most. The slight stubble of his beard only made the pleasure more intense. I grabbed his hair and pulled myself up, rocking my body in unison with his movements. He moved up to my breasts, taking time with each one, playing with them, teasing with his tongue, biting them until they were stiff, his medal dangling over them caressingly. One hand began exploring between my legs and found its way inside of me.

Again, he knew exactly how to please me, to tantalize me. I didn't think I could take it anymore. I removed his hand and pulled myself away from him, leaning down toward his midriff and taking him in my mouth. He let out a yelp. I kept looking in his eyes. He closed his as he pushed my head down.

At last, he pulled me away, brought me up to him, turned me around and mounted me so that we were face to face. He took both of my arms and held them over my head and my legs automatically wrapped themselves around his waist. Before I could grab him and pull him to me he was inside me with a burst of passion I had never experienced. I was barely conscious I was so engulfed in pleasure and desire. It seemed that we were in constant motion, he on me and in me, me on him and taking him in, not a single part of each other's bodies went unexplored by our mouths, our tongues, our teeth. We clenched hands so tightly I thought they would break. Neither of us was aware of our cries, the noises we were making. He held out much longer than I expected him to. Sheer will and discipline, I suspect. He was waiting for me. When we did come together it was an endless explosion. Years of anguish came pouring out of him. It didn't stop. I came again and still he was moving inside of me. I wanted him to stay there forever.

The only thing he said was, "Sybilla, Sybilla," over and over again, savoring my name in his mouth. It took a while before we were spent. It was then that we both broke down. I heard a sharp intake of breath and then the tears began cascading down his cheeks and he was wracking with sobs. His whole body shook. I started crying too but quietly. Blessed release.

Afterward we lay together in each other's arms in silence, holding on as tightly as we could. He didn't stop caressing me with a tenderness I had never known. It was then that the realization hit me. I had experienced the divine. What we had done was not only not a sin, it was sacred. I understood the true meaning of love. I also believed that God had sent us to be together. I have never been so sure of anything in my life.

I looked at Fitz and saw that his eyelids were drooping. "Don't leave me," he pleaded sleepily. "Please don't ever leave me."

I didn't know whether he was talking to me or to God.

With that he fell into a deep slumber. I waited for a few minutes and then quietly got up and put on my clothes. I hung his on the back of the chair, covered him with a blanket, turned out the desk lamp and, before leaving, took the note about the unicorn cup and slipped out the door.

Thursday

FITZ WOKE UP WITH A START at nine the next morning having slept through the night. Light was peeking through the curtains. He blinked a few times as he looked around the room, trying to remember where he was. He was lying naked on top of the bedspread with a blanket over him. His clothes were hanging on the back of the chair. He felt a sense of almost unrecognizable well-being. He let out a contented sigh before acknowledging that he was a bit disoriented.

He turned over and saw the bottle of Jameson on top of the desk. In his half dream state a vision was coming back to him in a confused jumble of images. There was the unicorn cup, there was a silvery laugh, a flash of shiny brown hair, a feeling of heat rising in his belly, a leap of faith, a glimmer of two pale bodies entwined, then a chemical reaction, a combustion, elation, then darkness.

What had happened to Sybilla? Where was she? Had she left him? He jumped off the bed and pulled open the curtains. It had been raining and the wind was whistling through the trees. The air was now misty, foggy, and gray. Soft. He looked frantically toward the door and then began to calm down. She had obviously left when he fell asleep to go to her own room. He was mortified. *What a great lover*, he thought to himself. Slam, bam, thank you ma'am had not been his usual style. He had been known in the old days for being as good at *après*-fuck as the deed itself. He was a champion cuddler. It got them every time.

Sybilla. The magical maiden with the unicorn. Sybilla, the purveyor of all joy. Sybilla of the brilliant, original luminous mind. His brain was a tangle of emotions, ecstasy, love, adoration, gratitude, fear, confusion, and guilt. He had forgotten that he had signed up for confession with Father Schmidt at ten. He thought that confession was a scam, another of his conflicts with the Church. Although he hadn't voiced this one. Yet. He certainly wasn't going to confess anything real. Besides, he had Father Joseph. God knows what he was going to tell him the next day when he had his last session with him. He would have to debate that later with himself.

It was too late to cancel confession. He'd just have to go and make up some sin he didn't commit or lie about one he did. He jumped in the shower reluctantly, not wanting to wash away her scent which permeated the room, his bed, his hair. He had no choice. He was damp with sweat and if he could smell her on himself, so could others.

He brushed his teeth, the effects of the whiskey had made his mouth dry, never mind what it had done to his head. He threw on some clean jeans, a T-shirt, and a hunter green Irish knit sweater.

He dashed up the stairs and arrived at the door of the tiny cubicle just in time. Father Schmidt was awaiting him. Fitz took an instant dislike to him. He looked younger than Fitz, but with an older affect.

He was thin with a bony, bald head, sharp beak for a nose, suspicious eyes, and thin lips which had never seen a smile. Right out of the Inquisition. Fitz felt Father Schmidt was judging him before he opened his mouth. And if Father Schmidt had only known where his mouth had been the night before he would have lit the torch on Fitz right then and there.

"Your Grace," he said with what seemed like a slight smirk on his face as he bowed unctuously to Fitz. Fitz debated, then did not invite him to call him by his name as he had with Father Joseph.

"Father Schmidt," said Fitz, not bowing.

Father Schmidt beckoned him to one of the two chairs, separated by a small table with a lamp. On the wall facing them was a crucifix.

Fitz crossed himself. "In the name of the Father, and of the Son, and of the Holy Spirit. Amen," he said. "Bless me Father for I have sinned. It has been six months since my last confession. These are my sins."

Father Schmidt waited.

Now what? thought Fitz. He had to come up with something good which would satisfy the inquisitor that he was adequately sinful.

"My sins, Father, are those of pride, of hubris, of vanity. I am well-known and somewhat of a celebrity. I like the attention too much." He was damned well not going to elaborate. Father Schmidt knew exactly what he was talking about.

Father Schmidt's eyes gleamed.

"And I am truly sorry for all of my sins."

"You understand your sins all too well," said Father Schmidt.

Professional to professional.

"You also know that pride is the sin from which all others arise."

Dramatic pause. "Your penance is to stay out of the public eye for six months. No interviews, no speeches, no public appearances except for your official duties." Wham! He got Fitz where he lived. He knew it, too. "You may pray the act of contrition."

After Fitz had done so, Father Schmidt said the prayer of absolution and made the sign of the cross.

"Amen," said Fitz.

"Give thanks to the Lord for he is good," said Father Schmidt. "His mercy endures forever. Your sins are forgiven. Go in peace."

"Thanks be to God," murmured Fitz. Then continued, "O my God, I am heartily sorry for having offended thee, and I detest all my sins because I dread the loss of heaven and the pains of hell, but most of all because they have offended thee, my God, who art all good and deserving of all my love, I firmly resolve, with the help of thy grace, to confess my sins, to do penance, and to mend my life. Amen."

Father Schmidt stood. Fitz stood as well. They nodded to each other. Father Schmidt couldn't hide the grin on his face. Fitz walked out of the cubicle, and down the hall to his room.

"Prick," he said under his breath.

Fitz was ravenous. And he hadn't had his morning run. He stopped off in the dining room and helped himself to a full breakfast. Orange juice. Hard boiled eggs. Yogurt, cereal with a banana, toast with apple butter. And coffee! He had never craved coffee more. He went back for another piece of toast, a second cup of coffee. Sybilla hadn't come.

He needed to pray. He hated running on a full stomach. Maybe he would just walk down to the river instead. He thought he might pray about his vanity. Wasn't that what Father Joseph had asked him that first day? What's going on in your prayers? It was the right question.

Although Father Schmidt had pissed him off, it was Fitz who had brought up that he was vain.

But first there was one thing he had to do. He had to write to Sybilla.

He walked slowly down the stairs to his room, hoping not to encounter her. He wasn't ready yet. He opened his door and surveyed the tossed bed, the clothes heaped on the chair, the half-empty bottle of Jameson. Carl Jung's unicorn cup. The magic cup. It had done its work last night. He moved the chair back where it belonged and sat at the desk to write. He pulled out his stationary and stared at it for a bit, frozen. There was so much to say. And so little he felt he needed to say. Hadn't she known everything he was feeling? He had filled her up with everything he had in every way. He didn't have the words, but his old mate Yeats did.

He put pen to paper.

"And thereupon his bounty gave what now
can shake more blossom from autumnal chill
than all my bursting springtime knew.
Meet me at the barn at 4 p.m.—F"

He stuffed it in the envelope. He formed the letters of her name on it. Hesitating at first, he kissed it, then slipped it under her door.

He was about to set out for his walk when he checked his phone to make sure there were no more epistles from the Vatican. Nothing but an email from his best mate and number two at the Archbishopric, Tommy O'Toole.

Tommy was the only person he could talk to, the only person who knew everything. He and Tommy had been at Trinity together, they had played rugby together. Tommy was the world's greatest goalie. He and Tommy had formed the band The A.O.H. together, he on guitar, Tommy on the piano. They had lived the debauched life together. Then, miraculously, they had entered the seminary at the same time. Now the two were inseparable.

The note and the Irish weather lightened his mood. Not raining, not drizzling, the air gently misted around his head and face. There was a reason they called it soft. It was tender. Wearing his dark green windbreaker, he felt embraced by it. It reminded him so of his childhood, walking the lanes of Glendalough. He closed his eyes and he was back in it again as if he had never left. The meadows with the cows grazing, the bales of hay, the woods in front of him, the river, all immersed him in a sense of peace. And yet since he had been here, since he had seen her, there had been no peace. There had been nothing but white noise. It had sometimes even felt as if he were losing his balance.

Pouring all of his feelings out to Father Joseph had certainly been cathartic, something he had needed to do for a long time. However, it had left him in a state of agitated exhaustion as well as relief. His prayers—he had definitely been praying—were garbled, inchoate, distracted. And last night, last night with Sybilla had left him with a myriad of emotions. Now he was determined to have a serious talk with God. He had been getting mixed messages from the Almighty and he needed some clarity.

He walked past the old barn overlooking the river. Would she show up at four? Was he crazy to have asked her? He half hoped she wouldn't come. He was so enmeshed in his own musings that he almost forgot to take a look inside the barn. He had to make sure their fated assignation would have at least a modicum of comfort. He stepped up the rickety stairs which led down an even more rickety hallway. Maybe this was a huge mistake. What if the barn fell down on top of them in the middle of their tryst?

Off to the right was a dark, musty room, filled with dead leaves and cobwebs and some old tools. The room gave off to the covered outdoor pen near the river. It was marginally acceptable. There was an old rake in the corner with which he could clean a spot for them. He would have to go back to the guest house and get a blanket. It wasn't freezing but it was definitely damp, and they couldn't just sit (or lie) on the rough-hewn floor. He would wait to get the blanket until he finished with God. His soul needed cleaning and warming up before he could attend to the barn.

Pulling up his hood he walked down to the river, making his way to the place on the bank where he had been the day before. The rock, the fallen tree with its exposed twisted roots, Awsheen and Finn McCool. Awsheen needed a little work. He found a sharp stone on the water's edge and etched two wide eyes into the hard rock, then carved a big grin for his mouth. There was a pile of fallen red leaves near the tree beside him which he piled on the top of Awsheen's head for hair.

"My mate," he said and reflexively hugged the rock, his eyes welling up. He glanced over at the mangled roots. "Finn," he said. "You're not alone, you know. She's here with us."

It pained him to look at Finn. He had always been a bit jealous of the way Dierdre had adored him. More than that, though, Finn's contorted limbs reminded him of the X-rays he'd seen of Dierdre's brain when the glioblastoma had metastasized. He shuddered. Maybe this wasn't the best place for prayer after all. On the other hand, what could be a better spot? He was home. The closest he had ever felt to God was in Glendalough on the river's edge. That was where he had done his most serious praying. When his parents were fighting, when his mum died, then his da. When he turned away from God before he went to Trinity. When he finally decided to dedicate his life to God. When he met Dierdre. When she got sick. When she died. When he began to turn away again. When he was rescued and embraced by God. And when he rededicated himself to God.

In the last twenty years, disappointingly, he had not had those kinds of seminal moments with his Creator. It was odd, really. For some reason they had both taken each other for granted. God was always going to be there for him. He was always going to be there for God. There was something different going on now. He couldn't quite define it but he knew that things had changed.

He needed to move toward the change. He needed metanoia. He had been headed for a breakdown for a long time, repressing it from himself and from God. It was time for the metamorphosis so that he could begin to heal. He had come to this place, the retreat, to be silent, to find clarity. To find peace. He had come to this river to be still. There was a saying, "May that which is still be that in which your mind delights." He wanted to find that delight again. He had always considered Father Richard Rohr's advice that centering prayer was a crucial remedy for one's fragmented condition, and that solitude, silence, and stillness were important in helping us "discern the voice of God, uncover our true self and live a life of meaning and purpose." And yet he had veered from that path into one of extreme agitation and confusion. He thought of a line by one of his favorite Irish poets, John O'Donohue: "When the canvas frays/in the currach of thought/ And a stain of ocean/Blackens beneath you, May there come across the waters/A path of yellow moonlight/To bring you safely home."

He had to find his way back to God again. Here. Now.

"Dear God," he prayed out loud. At least it was a start.

But he was stuck. Maybe a conversation would be better. Something a little more informal. Something like his conversation with Father Joseph. They had been on pretty good terms, he and God. A lot of people didn't find God that accessible. Somehow, he was too unembodied for them. They related better to Jesus. Jesus had a face. Jesus had a story. Jesus had suffered just like they had. On the other hand, he felt he had a deeper connection to God. God was the father he never had.

"God," he said out loud again, "we need to talk."

He took in his surroundings: the river rolling by, the leaves falling gently, the mist settling on his shoulders. He took in deep breaths. He took in the silence. If he wanted to be with God, to know God at this moment, he had to do it in silence. He let the silence engulf him. He surrendered to the silence.

"I want to talk to you about love," he said after a long while. "All of my life I have been preached to about love. I have preached love. I have preached that the foundation of everything is love. I have preached that God is love, I have preached love thy neighbor as thyself. Love is patient, love is kind. Lest all you do be done in love. I have preached Agape and Philia and Storge, and Eros. Over and over again, I have even importuned my congregations, 'Beloved, let us know another, for love is from God and whoever loves has been born of God and knows God.' I'm confounded. I don't know what love means any more. Help me to understand. I have loved many people, many things, many places, many ideas, and I have loved them all in different ways. Never have I considered any of those ways to love wrong. But the Church, your Church, in your name has condemned the love we know as Eros. Certainly, Eros is forbidden to those of us who have taken our vows to you and to others outside marriage. But why? It doesn't make any sense to me anymore. That's why I wrote my book. I tried not to criticize the Church's position on celibacy but simply to question the wisdom of it. I wasn't true to myself when I wrote that. I am angry with the Church for many reasons. I am also angry at you. Mostly I am angry with myself. I've tried to protect the Church, to not denounce the atrocities of the child sexual abuse in a way that would embarrass you. I tried to be delicate about the Church's position on women and homosexuality. I even tried to rationalize the Church's position on celibacy. Though I haven't kept my vows, I have kept the faith, but I am not sure how much longer I can contain my outrage at the hypocrisy. And all in your name, God. I have loved you with all of my heart, but you are letting this happen. I need you to explain to me, to help me understand why because I am anguished by my confusion and by the decisions I feel I am going to have to make. What is happening in the Church is anathema to everything Jesus, your son, stood for, died for. It's anathema to everything I have stood for, believed in, devoted my life to, because of you. None of these issues has anything to do with love. Not love as I know it. Not love as you have shown me. Not love as Jesus gave his life for."

 He thought of Dierdre as she danced merrily in the meadow. He thought of Sybilla as she had wrapped her body around him last night. He had loved Dierdre with all of his heart. He loved Sybilla. He was in love with Sybilla. He couldn't imagine living in a world without her. If it was possible in such a short time, he believed he loved her with all of his heart and always would. It was not the same as his love for God. It was a different kind of love. His love for Dierdre had been pure and innocent and good. There was never anything about it that could be condemned by anyone who truly believed in love. His love for Sybilla was something more profound. The beauty of it, the ecstasy, the depth, the unimaginable joy of it was all-consuming. Nothing could persuade him that anything he had done with Sybilla was wrong, that anything he felt for her wasn't true to everything he believed. Nothing could persuade him otherwise that everything he had done with his calling was true to what he believed. What he had with Sybilla was holy. What he had with the Church was not. His love for God was infinite but not tangible. What would his life be going forward if Sybilla were not in it? What would his life be going forward if God were not in it? If he had to choose between them at this moment, it would be impossible.

"God," he beseeched. "My faith in you has never wavered, even though I have been so deeply troubled by the actions of the Church. I have pondered it, struggled with it, wrestled with it and always, always have come back to it. I don't want to lose my faith. I would be an empty man without it. I believe you brought Dierdre to me. You brought her to me for a reason. My love for her was inseparable from my love for you. When you took her from me I was shocked. I believed I had sinned against you and I've spent the better part of my life paying penance for it, trying to redeem myself, pledging my faith to you as strongly as I can. Yet I never understood it. I still don't. Was it a test? If so, it was harsh. Now I believe you have brought Sybilla to me. For a reason. But if this is another test, I don't want it. I don't want to be Job. I can't endure it. Are you tempting me to teach me a lesson again? To cement my faith in you forever? Will you take her away from me, the way you did Dierdre? I can't believe you would do that to me again. I believe you are a benevolent God, and you are the one who has taught me that the foundation of love is all. I have tried to live my life that way and I will continue to do so. With your blessing."

He paused for a moment and then bowed his head. Even though it had been a conversation, not a prayer, he said, "Amen."

Years ago, he had spent some time in Jerusalem, studying Judaism and Islam with the Rabbis and the Imams. He had loved arguing and debating with the Rabbis and their intellectual rigor. He had also been entranced by the Adhan, the Muslim call to prayer which resounded throughout the Old City five times a day. The haunting devotional made him feel closer to God than any hymn he had ever known. He had learned it from a muezzin. It always filled him with awe.

Now he stood. He was stiff from sitting in the same position for such a long time. He shook out his limbs and walked to the edge of the river. It was still misting a little. He had no idea what time it was. Lifting his arms to the sky, he belted out the words to the call to prayer in a deep sing-song voice. "God is the Greatest. God is the greatest."

He waited for a moment, half expecting God to respond. He didn't know what he was hoping for. Thunder? Lightening? A loud voice? He smiled to himself. He was still a child of God after all.

He started walking back up the path to the barn.

Halfway there he felt a rustle and looked down at his feet. There on the ground in front of him lay an eagle feather. It had not been there before. He would have noticed it. He reached down to pick it up. He stroked its perfectly formed gray and white stripes with wonder. How had it gotten there? He hadn't seen the bird. Was it a sign? No. That was too hokey. On the other hand, what about religion wasn't? What did it mean? He knew that the eagle represented the highest, the strongest, and the bravest. It also represented the holiest.

I woke caressing my body. I ran my hands over my breasts and down my arms, stopping between my legs. I was still mostly asleep, not quite aware of where I was, what I was doing. I stretched and yawned and purred. I smiled. Eudaimonia. Aristotle's definition of happiness was something that had eluded me all of my life. Of course, I had had moments of joy, elation even. This was something different. This was a feeling of total serenity, of complete and permanent happiness. I rolled over and curled up around my pillow, thinking of going back to sleep to finish my delicious dream. It was the scent of him on my body, in my hair, that brought it all back. The night of lovemaking with Fitz. And it was lovemaking. I realized that I had never truly been made love to before. I had had intense and satisfying sex, especially in the beginning with Spraig. Yet, nothing like this. I relived the entire evening with him, going over every erotic detail, every euphoric feeling. I was astounded by how in love with him I felt. I believed he felt the same way. He had to. I could barely contain myself, so obsessed with the thought of our love that I never even considered what our future might be. It didn't even occur to me. I just knew in my heart that we were meant to be together and that we would be together. Anything else was not possible.

I jumped out of bed, ready to start the day and to see him as soon as I could. It was later than I thought, almost ten. Lauds had long passed. Clearly, I was never going to make it to Lauds again. I had to shower and get something to eat before my last session with Father Joseph. When I opened the curtains I saw that it was misting outside and the air coming in the window was much colder than yesterday. Given that my underwear had been exposed yesterday in the river, I didn't want to take a chance in not having a sexy pair of underwear today. I pulled a pair of mauve lace panties and matching bra out of my suitcase and put them on. Then I chose a light blue cashmere turtleneck, jeans, and rain boots. A touch of pale lip gloss, the tiniest trace of eyeliner, a brush through my hair, which was still redolent of him, and I was ready to go.

No sign of Fitz upstairs. But the cat, that awful cat which had been prowling around, had stationed itself in front of me, its back arched and a menacing look on its face. I couldn't stand cats. Strange, since as Sybilla, a sorceress, one would think I would have my own familiar, my own tool, in my practice of magic. For me, it most certainly would not be a cat! Cats were untrustworthy. They couldn't be counted on. For me they represented black magic. I turned to avoid it and watched it slink away.

There was barely time for a yogurt before I was to meet with Father Joseph. What a difference a day makes, as they say. I bounced into his room and greeted him with a big grin. He seemed surprised at my joyful demeanor, so different from when last we met. He stood up when I entered and waited for me to take my seat.

"Good morning, Father," I said cheerfully, I glanced at the ubiquitous tissue box. "Well," I said. "I definitely will not be needing those today!"

"So, to what do we ascribe this change of heart?" he asked, clearly amused.

"Silence. Prayer. Meditation," I said. I may as well have winked.

"That was fast."

"No, really," I insisted. "I've been doing a lot of thinking."

"And?"

"I've decided to stop feeling sorry for myself and let go of my anger and pain. I've decided to be more forgiving."

"Sounds like you've been reading too many self-help books."

"I thought you would be pleased."

He didn't say anything. Just looked at me knowingly. Obviously, I couldn't possibly tell him the truth. I stuttered a bit, not really able to think of what to say.

I was relieved when Father Joseph said, "When last we left off, you were married to a man you didn't love who was infertile. What's changed?"

"Nothing."

"I'm not buying it."

I squirmed in my seat. Father Joseph got up and walked over to the window and stared out at the willow tree.

He turned to me finally and said, "I'm here for you, Sybilla."

Something about his tone inspired me to reflect. I wanted to wallow in my newfound happiness, not return to my old misery. But he had me cornered.

"Spraig started cheating on me," I said.

"How did you find out?"

Spraig wanted me to know. He left clues everywhere. Lipstick on his collar. American Express bills from Tiffany's. Hotel bills. Late nights at the office. Whispering into his cell phone when I was in the other room. Phone calls in the middle of the night. It would've actually been ludicrous if it hadn't been so sad.

He turned on me. He became critical and judgmental. Everything I did was wrong. He said mean and hurtful things. My name was not safe in his mouth. He actually called me a bitch. He didn't want to make love to me anymore. It's not exactly that I was desperate to have sex with him, but I did need to be held, to have some kind of intimacy. Every once in a while, if he'd had too much to drink, he would pounce on me, but it was hardly what I would call satisfying. I became so lonely. I lost my confidence. But mostly I was grieving for the fact that I would never have children and the loss of what had been my marriage. We went to a shrink a few times. That only ended up in his being defensive and blaming me for blaming him for being infertile. He accused me of robbing his manhood, of making him feel like a worthless failure. I never, never did that. I was so careful to do exactly the opposite. To build him up and tell him how fabulous and sexy and handsome he was. The fact was though, that I was believing it less and less as his treatment of me became almost intolerable. I brought up his affairs. He denied everything, even when I presented him with evidence. He just said I was paranoid. He was totally gaslighting me. Not for the first time, I dabbled in the occult.

I went back to my astrologers, psychics, shamans, palmists, and tarot card readers. I got hooked on well-being. I exercised like crazy: Barre3, Pilates, aerobics, yoga, hiking, swimming, dancing, anything that would make me sweat. I went to spas. I had stone massages and facials. I tried reiki. I went to Zendos for Buddhist meditations. I even went to a hypnotist. Without telling Spraig, I had my eggs frozen.

I slept nine hours a night. I rarely drank except for an occasional prosecco with pomegranate juice (it could have easily gone the other way). I ate fruits and vegetables and nuts and lean chicken and fish. I had manicures and pedicures, makeup lessons, highlights, and a new, shorter, younger-looking haircut. I even got a Brazilian wax. Anything to make me feel beautiful and sexy and desirable. I totally pampered myself. I went to Town Shop Lingerie store on West 82nd and got fitted for new sets of sexy Empreinte bras and bikini panties. I sprayed on my perfume, Sortilège, whenever I went out the door. I took long walks in Central Park and would spend hours at The Cloisters reading in the garden and looking at the unicorn tapestries when the weather was nice. I took an Enneagram test and found that I was a Number 2. The Helper. The worst-case scenario: clinging, dependent, victim, martyr, overly possessive, resentful, suffocating. I began visiting my parents in Boston or the Vineyard a lot. I went to Spetses without Spraig. I began working longer hours just to relieve myself of the anguish. I got to the point where I really didn't care anymore. I had fallen out of love with him. In fact, I almost hated him. Even so, I hadn't really contemplated divorce. And he never mentioned the word.

My book project was the thing that saved me. I started work on it about nearly a year ago when Duncan Cohen, my old professor of mythology at Harvard, called me out of the blue and asked me to tour the unicorn tapestries at the Cloisters in New York City. It was synchronicity at its most intense, something which would become increasingly relevant to me as time passed. I had always been fascinated by the unicorn, but I had never known why. When I was a child my mother took me to see the six famous tapestries "The Lady and the Unicorn" in the Cluny Museum in Paris. The museum was near where my grandmother lived, where my mother had grown up, in a *hôtel particulier* on the Rue du Bac on the Left Bank. Every time we went to visit "Mimi" I would insist on going there. As I got older, I found I was being drawn to the Cluny where I would visit by myself for hours. It wasn't until I got to college that I began to study art, religion, classics, and mythology, and though I remained interested in the unicorns, my interests were diverging into myriad other areas which eventually led me to journalism in New York.

It was only this past year, because of Duncan, that I came back to the unicorn again. We spent hours examining the mystical tapestries, he, ever the teacher, explaining the Christology of the unicorn, the unicorn as a symbol of Christ. Later, our lunches ran into dinners and many bottles of very good French wine. Duncan invited me to visit him in his stone cottage in Scotland, on Loch Fyne. "Your favorite gay Scottish Jew," he joked. He took me to visit his family's house on the Isle of Jura. We talked about the magic of the stones and the myths of Scottish mysticism. He had gotten interested in the unicorn because it was Scotland's official national animal. He loved the contrasting symbology of the unicorn, not only as purity and innocence but masculinity and power as well. He was convinced that, even though I had very little Scottish blood on my father's side, that I, Sybilla, was a nicnevin, a Scottish witch or fairy queen. My sorcery was going to waste he felt. I should put it to good use. He introduced me to a new way of seeing the world. I had never understood the word until then. It was metanoia, a transformative change of heart.

"Metanoia," said Father Joseph, sitting up straighter. "One of my favorite words. One of the most important things that can happen to someone. If it's for the good, you are fortunate."

"It's working for me."

"The book project?"

"The unicorn as an idea of magic. When I was little, before I lapsed, I loved the magic of the Church. Since I lost that I've been looking for it most of my life. I found it in the unicorn. What really excited me about it was the idea that people like Yeats and Carl Jung and Plato had the same obsession. They were all religious in their own ways but not traditionally."

"Say more about this."

"Yeats was all about the occult and the magic of the unicorn. He saw it as a symbol which could open doors to the collective mind. He had a book plate with a unicorn on it. Plato's riddle of being and nonbeing, reality and illusion, fascinated me although I have to admit I don't totally understand it. The unicorn exists because how could it not, certainly in the world of ideas. Plato is a little obtuse for me. I much prefer Aristotle. He was into happiness. Carl Jung speaks to me. He was a brilliant psychologist. He really did understand the human mind as well as the collective unconscious. He understood the deep need of every human to find the magic in the world. He said of his unicorn cup: 'My tankard tells me/speaking in mute silence/what I must become.' He believed the essence of the unicorn was the bestower of strength, health, and life; the image of the spirit. The thing I love most about Jung is his final words. 'Let's have a really good red wine tonight.' How can you not love Carl Jung?"

"You won't get an argument from me."

"It was thanks to Duncan that I wrote my piece on the unicorn for *The New Yorker*. That led to a book contract which I am working on now."

"I'm aware of your success," he said. "The McArthur Genius award."

"I don't feel like much of a genius right now."

"Genius is in the eye of the beholder. Tell me more about what fascinates you so about the unicorn?"

"Its beauty, its innocence, its power. Plus the fact that the Christian Church, at least until recently, believed that the unicorn represented Christ. Christ was pure. Christ could only be captured by a virgin. Christ died at the hands of nonbelievers. The tapestries at the Cloisters and the Cluny illustrate that symbolism perfectly. Yet all of us can see something different in the unicorn. We can give it our own interpretation. The unicorn is as personal to me as God may be to others. For me the unicorn is love in its purest form. It is a love I truly believe in and truly aspire to."

"A love you have not found?"

Was he probing? Did he suspect something?

I shifted uneasily. He let it go.

"Tell me," he asked. "What will you do?"

I didn't answer at first because I honestly didn't know. How could I?

"About what?"

"About your marriage."

"I don't know."

"Sybilla," he said. "There's something you're not telling me."

"I don't know. I don't know." I started to cry. "I don't know."

He sat there watching. He didn't come over to comfort me the way he had last time. This was different. We both knew it.

I cried until I was out of breath. I couldn't look at him.

At last, I lifted my eyes and met his. They were clear and blue and deep. They were welcoming. There was no judgment there.

"I've met someone," I said haltingly.

He nodded. He knew I had told him the truth.

"I have fallen in love with a man who is unavailable and unattainable."

I had no idea what he would say, how he would react.

When he spoke, his voice was rich with emotion.

"True love," he said, "is unconquerable and irresistible, and it goes on gathering power and spreading itself, until eventually it transforms everyone whom it touches."

I hoped he was giving me his blessing but I couldn't tell.

"I think the silence has been good for you. I believe it has awakened you to the presence of God, or however you want to describe it. It is freeing you. Your happiness has already been given to you."

He stood up. I stood up. I thought I detected his eyes misting over. He bent his head in a bow of farewell.

"Go with God," he said.

I made the same gesture and walked out the door.

I barely made it back to my room I was so undone. I couldn't believe I had admitted to Father Joseph that I was in love. All I wanted to do was just collapse on the bed and try to deal with the bewilderment in my head. I had told Father Joseph the truth. I really didn't know what I was going to do. I didn't know what Fitz was going to do. As I entered my room, I saw the envelope on the floor. I grabbed it, slammed the door behind me, ran to the bed and ripped it open. It was an invitation to meet him at the barn at four. I could barely contain myself. I was desperate to see him.

The lunch bell rang and I jumped. Would he be there? How would we behave with each other? Could we hide the electricity? I didn't care. I threw the letter on the bed and dashed up the stairs and into the dining room, practically colliding with Arianthe. She looked at me askance, her frizzy hair tucked under the collar of her baggy sweater. She knew! Of course she didn't know. But then Deedee looked at me inquiringly, her dyed blonde hair tucked under her black velvet headband. Oh no! This was ridiculous. It was when poor Dave, his stomach hanging over his belt, glanced at me with a sad, hangdog expression that I realized they all knew. Only Krish seemed oblivious. *Get a grip, Sybilla, you're sounding like a mean girl.* There was no way they could know. On the other hand, what about the cries of passion in the night? Not possible. Only Krish was on our floor, and he was at the other end of the hall. Yes, but the other three were upstairs and I didn't know which rooms they were in. Maybe one above Fitz's. Oh God! However, even if one had heard, they couldn't tell anyone else because it was a silent retreat. I was so focused on who knew what and when that I didn't realize for a moment that Fitz wasn't there. I was deflated and relieved. At least I could eat in peace, and I was ravenous.

I headed to the counter and filled my plate with baked tilapia, yellow rice, and broccoli, wolfed it down, and then went back for lemon squares for dessert. It must have taken me all of fifteen minutes to finish my lunch and I headed back downstairs to wait for midday prayer. Surely Fitz would be there. Where else could he be? I would have some time now to process my conversation with Father Joseph. It was not to be. When I got back to the room I made the mistake of checking my phone. There was an email from Spraig. I almost didn't read it but then I was too curious not to. I wondered if he was picking up vibes from what was going on here.

"What the hell is going on?" He began. He never disappointed. "I've texted you several times. No response. We really need to talk. This little snit of yours is not playing well. Yes, I know it's been a difficult time for both of us but we're married and we love each other. We can work things out. I can't believe you're actually being silent on your 'silent retreat.' Have you gotten the hots for some monk!!!????? Ha! What are you doing all day there anyway? Praying!!!!?????? I'd have to see it to believe it. I just don't get it. How's the food there? Michelin 3 stars? I've been working my ass off. Had great interviews this week. Gotten raves. Not that you would be interested. I emceed the Committee to Protect Journalists, moderated a panel at the Council on Foreign Relations, had lunch at Michael's with the guys, played squash every day at the Racquet Club. What time do you get in Saturday afternoon? Why don't I take you out for a romantic dinner at Caravaggio. I'll order a bottle of Roederer Cristal Rose and we can plan our future together. Actually, I was thinking. How would you feel about renewing our vows? We could have a big party in Southampton in front of all of our friends. It would be fun. I really do miss you, Sybilla. And yes, I do love you. Spraig"

I sighed. Poor Spraig. He was probably the least introspective person I had ever known. I don't think I had ever felt sorrier for him than I did at that moment. But it was too late. For him and for me.

"Dear Spraig," I began, then crossed out the "Dear." "Spraig," I wrote, leaning against my pillow. "Sorry I haven't been very communicative. I really am trying to stay silent and off the grid. It's been good. I've had a chance to do a lot of thinking. You are right. We've had a rough time of it. I believe you when you say you want to try to work things out. The question is . . . can we? It seems to me that there is a lot of brokenness in both of us and I'm not at all sure we can put the pieces back together. We have tried before. It didn't work. There's no trust left between us. I came down here as a last resort. You say you love me but you have an odd way of showing it. I don't feel cherished by you anymore. I don't feel beloved. I need to feel beloved on this earth. S."

As soon as I hit send, I turned off my phone, put it on the desk, and started up to the chapel for midday prayer. Would Fitz show up? In a way it would be better if he didn't. I didn't need the distraction right now.

I took my usual seat in the back of the chapel. They were all there. All four of them. He was not.

I hadn't really had time to distill my session with Father Joseph or my email with Spraig. "What are you doing there all day anyway? Praying!!!!??????" Spraig had asked disparagingly. Well, yes, actually. I certainly felt like praying now. I knelt as the monks came in. I crossed myself.

"Dear God," I prayed, without any reticence or embarrassment. "I need your help. I came here not knowing who I was or what I wanted. Now I do. You have given me the gift of clarity and for that I praise you. But the clarity has brought me both joy and despair. I now know that I want Fitz. I want to love and cherish him for the rest of my life. I want to marry him. I want to have his babies. I have never encountered the ecstasy, the closeness to the divine that I have with him, not even when I believed in you. I am giving you the benefit of the doubt here. One thing I do not doubt is that you brought us together and you wouldn't have done that if you didn't want us to love each other in the most sacred way. What I worry about is Fitz. He has devoted his life to you. He is already married to you. I am married to Spraig. I do realize that I can break my vows to Spraig a lot more easily than Fitz can break his vows to you. For Fitz, divorce is almost unthinkable, especially if he believed he would have to give you up if he gave up the Church. I don't want to be the cause of his 'divorce' any more than I'm sure he doesn't want to be the cause of mine. I have fallen out of love with Spraig. Knowing Fitz's devotion and passion I can't imagine him ever falling out of love with you. If he left the Church, it would have to be with the understanding that he is not leaving you. I would rather die than be the cause of his guilt or sadness. I couldn't bear it if one day he were to blame me, or be angry with me for his decision to leave the Church. I only want to be with him if he wholeheartedly wants to be with me until death do us part. Please understand me, God. I don't want to come between you and Fitz. I want you to make room in his heart so that he can love us both equally. I also don't want him to be angry with you for keeping him from me. As I see it, God, we could have a win-win situation but only if he comes to that realization on his own. You must know that I will never love anyone as I do him. I will never leave him. I will never be with another man again. I am his and I am yours too, if you will allow us to be together. Only you can make it happen. I have faith that you will. Thank you, dear God, for bringing him to me. You will never regret it. He will be a greater, more forceful presence in this world if he is filled with joy, filled with both our love. Much more so than if he were angry, bitter, guilty, lonely, and sad. Let him fulfill his potential as your representative. Let me fulfill mine as his loving partner. Together we can do so much good. In your name. Amen."

I found myself weeping with gratitude as the service was ending.

I think I actually believed that God was listening. In any case, I felt heard. I waited until the others had left the chapel and then slowly walked to the guest house. I had to pull myself together before I met Fitz at the barn. Back in my room I lay on my bed and stared at the ceiling, at once emotionally exhausted and emotionally invigorated.

It was twenty minutes to four when I prepared to leave. I could see a steady drizzle out the window, so I put on my boots and a warmer jacket, grabbed my umbrella, and started down toward the river. The weather had changed from a balmy summer day to cold, damp, and rainy. Even the cows looked miserable, the haystacks were waterlogged. Fitz probably loved it. Real Irish weather.

I was more nervous about seeing him than I had been since I got here. I didn't know what to expect from him. Would he have had second thoughts? Was he asking to meet with me to tell me this had to stop? Was he going to tell me he loved me? My mind was churning with anticipation and apprehension. There was an old tale called *The Lady or the Tiger* which I could never get out of my mind. It was about a lady who was in love with a knight. When he won his jousting match she had to decide what was to become of him. Unable to have him herself, she could choose to send him to the tiger to be eaten or send him to another beautiful woman to wed. I always thought that was a really tough choice. Without being overly dramatic, Fitz and I had similar choices to make.

I got to the barn just in time to miss the deluge.

I wasn't quite sure where I was to go. There was an entrance to the side with a covered hallway which I took. It was so dilapidated that I was a little afraid to enter. It looked like it was about to collapse at any minute.

Gingerly, I made my way down the hall until I came to a door on the right, on the river side. It was slightly cracked. I hesitated for a moment, not knowing what I would find, then pushed it open. It was dark and musty inside the windowless room but not terribly cold.

When I adjusted to the dimness, I saw him. He was sitting on the floor cross legged on a blanket, looking like a Buddhist monk meditating. He had a small paper plate to the side with several lemon squares, clearly pilfered from the dining room, and two Styrofoam cups of steaming hot tea. Facing him was another blanket rolled up. He had placed his backpack and jacket behind him. On the other side was his phone. The flashlight gave the room a slight glow. Music was playing. I recognized the singer immediately. It was Shirley Horn, one of the greatest jazz singers of all time and one of my favorites. Slow and seductive, her honeyed voice permeated the room. "My, As Time Goes By." I felt an immediate seizing in my heart. Casablanca. Humphrey and Ingrid. "You must remember this. A kiss is just a kiss. A sigh is just a sigh." We know what happened to them. They gave each other up for the most noble of reasons. Had he planned this? Was he trying to send me a message? I couldn't imagine it. When he saw me, I froze. He stood. The expression on his face, the look in his eyes—it gave him away.

HE HADN'T SEEN HER SINCE he had fallen asleep in her arms. She was even more exquisite than he remembered. Her cheeks were pink and dripping with rain, her smile radiant. She left her umbrella open and put it aside, then pulled off her wet jacket and hood and tossed it in the corner he had swept earlier. Wordless, they faced each other.

Before he even realized what he was doing, he reached for her. He circled her, then pushed her up against the rickety wall, devouring her with his mouth. He couldn't stop himself. He wasn't even aware of the intensity of her response. All he knew was that he had never wanted any creature the way he wanted her. He grabbed her hair with one hand and pulled her head back, licking and biting her neck. She was letting out small gasps and clutching at him at the same time. One hand ran down her back and inside her tights, finding her and grasping her with his fingers. She was trying to wrap her legs around him but he pushed her away and pulled down her pants. He planted his mouth in her, still touching her inside until she began to writhe. He unzipped himself and easily plunged into her. She was ready for him. He grabbed her bare buttocks and lifted her up to him until her legs were wrapped around his waist. From somewhere he could hear the boards of the old building begin to creak. She was as avaricious as he was, biting and clawing at him. They were ravaging each other. He was afraid he wouldn't be able to hold out long enough to satisfy her, but she came first in a loud, almost anguished cry and he followed suit, still holding on, clutching her to him, holding her up against the wall, still rapacious for more.

    He pulled her off of him, fastened his pants, and carried her over to the blanket, laying her down and taking the other blanket to cover her from the chill. He lay down next to her, pulled the blanket over himself and lifted up her sweater to lick her breasts which hardened immediately. He could feel the same thing happening to him. They fucked each other again. And then again. Shirley Horn was still singing. The tea was cold. The lemon squares forgotten. The rain was softly dripping on the tin roof. It was darker outside. Fitz looked at his phone. It was five-thirty. Dinner was at six-thirty, barely enough time to get back and dry off. He had missed so many meals he didn't want people to get suspicious. Besides, it was getting colder rapidly. He showed her the time and motioned that they should go. He got up and zipped his pants and started to collect his belongings. She rose and pulled up her tights and straightened her clothes. He opened the door, helped her with her coat, still damp from the rain, and handed her the umbrella. Both of them were in such a daze that they forgot to kiss, forgot to bid each other farewell.

As soon as she left, he went out to the pen and poured out the tea, careful to put the cups and bags in his backpack. Leave no trace. He laid out the lemon squares for the critters, knowing they would be gone by morning. He rolled up the blankets and stuffed them in his backpack and put on his jacket and hood and set out for the guest house. He hadn't thought to bring an umbrella but it didn't matter. He was completely oblivious to the weather.

He was halfway back when he felt something hit him on the head. The rain had subsided. It definitely wasn't hail. He kept walking when another thing pinged him on the leg. He stared down at the road but it was dirt and gravel so he couldn't tell whether it had come from there or not. He thought it was strange. He ventured on when he got it on his behind. This was ridiculous! He was determined to find out what was going on. To his left was a large, rolled haystack. He would go behind it and watch to see what was happening. As he stepped behind the hay, there was Sybilla, ready to hurl another pebble at him.

"What the hell!" he mumbled to himself, and she immediately collapsed in a heap of giggles. "Vixen!" he said with a fake grimace and grabbed her and threw her to the ground and pinned her down. She burst out laughing and fought him off with no success. He kissed her playfully, then not so playfully.

Before they knew it, they were at it again, hidden by the haystack. When they had finished, he took her umbrella and held it over their heads as they lay in the sodden field. The rain had stopped. It was misting now. Soft again. As they were lying there, they heard a loud whoosh. As they looked up, they saw a murmuration of starlings, thousands of birds, flocking together in formation, swirling around the sky over the monastery in a gorgeous ballet of joy. They both gasped in awe. Fitz had only seen it once before. He had just taken his vows and was walking the meadow in the hills outside of Glendalough. It was as if the starlings were consecrating his ordination. He took it then as a hallowed sign. He took it the same way now.

They watched the flock and then Fitz sent Sybilla ahead so they wouldn't be spotted together. After she had gone in, he followed.

In his room, he took off his jacket and shook it, then toweled it off and hung it on the back of his desk chair to dry. He jumped in the shower, changed into his black turtleneck, and raced up the stairs, his hair still wet. Sybilla hadn't made it up yet. The others were already there. He felt guilty thinking of them as the "others." It seemed so condescending, so exclusive. He didn't intend it to mean that. It was just that he thought now of himself and Sybilla as one and they were "other," distinct from the two of them.

The Gregorian chants were playing more loudly than usual. A heavenly intervention. He could tell that Deedee was trying to flirt with him. He didn't want to meet her eyes but she was clearly preening for him. She kept trying to get his attention. After he had filled his plate with chicken salad, three bean salad, bread, and sat down, she got up and walked fetchingly toward the dessert table to get her peaches. She had on black velvet stretch pants and a white angora sweater; a little overdressed for the monastery. After a cursory glance around the room he couldn't help but notice that Arianthe had put on a tiny bit of lipstick and had tried to tame her wild hair to no avail. Krish was in his own world. Dave kept looking at the door, obviously waiting for Sybilla to arrive. *Poor bastard*, Fitz thought, as he tried not to stare at the door himself.

Sybilla dashed in just as everyone else was getting their dessert. Fitz had gone back for seconds, then dessert, so he would have an excuse to stay at the table. She looked glorious. Her face was flushed from sex and the cold. Her hair was still incriminatingly damp. She was wearing a loose slightly off the shoulder black cashmere sweater and black yoga pants. He took in his breath, his stomach contracted. He tried to avert his glance, but it was impossible. Nobody noticed. They were all staring at her. She illuminated the space.

Fitz felt like chanting himself. He wanted to bang his head on the table in supplication. He kept eating, feeling her move about the room, getting her plate, taking her place at the table. Nobody was leaving even though they had all finished eating. They all went back for more peaches. Fitz couldn't wait around any longer. It would have looked a bit suspicious. He tried not to look as he passed by her on his way out. He couldn't imagine, though, that anybody could be in the same room with them and not know.

Compline was at seven-thirty, but he decided to head over early and take a shot at praying. He felt he had already said his piece to God. But then, one is never finished talking to God. It was still drizzling but not as hard. He walked quickly up to the chapel, leaving his umbrella in the tiny vestibule and going directly to his seat, pausing to bow to the altar and cross himself. Before he knew it, he was on his knees.

He was alone. It was dark inside and the candles and pale lighting made it seem almost mystical. He sat back up on the bench. Oddly he didn't feel like praying. Meditation, rumination, were what he felt compelled to do. He needed to meditate on his future, not just with Sybilla but with the Church. He wanted to ruminate on the morality of the decisions he must make. He wasn't going to ask God for help or advice or guidance this time. Now it was up to him. He had been here for four days. Four days, not exactly in silence, not exactly in solitude or stillness either. All were prerequisites for a successful retreat. He had spent a considerable amount of his time in anguish as well as euphoria. He had spent all of his time at the monastery in a state of spiritual entropy. The order in his life, or at least what he had thought was order, had disintegrated into chaos. If he had hoped to find himself while here, he had failed, at least up until now. He only had one day left to reclaim his sanity. As usual he turned to Thomas Merton, the wisest of men. Merton had said, "What can we gain by sailing to the moon if we are not able to cross the abyss that separates us from ourselves. This is the most important of all voyages of discovery, and without it, all the rest are not only useless, but disastrous."

Sybilla was the moon. He had sailed to the moon but he had not yet been able to cross the abyss. He had to or he would be headed for disaster. He understood that. He hoped his last session with Father Joseph could help him sort things out, sort out his bewilderment at this newfound fervor for Sybilla which had become a replacement for the fervor he had always felt for God, for the Church.

He had a special mantra he always used for meditation. It was given to him by a Buddhist monk he befriended on one of his trips.

"Dove." The monk had laughed affectionately when he gave it to him, explaining that the dove was the symbol of peace and the Holy Spirit, and that he was always in flight, that he was innocent, adventurous, and good-natured. Fitz liked the mantra. It suited him. It worked for him. He chanted the mantra under his breath, "Dove, dove, dove," until he had almost hypnotized himself. He was in a trance. He was barely aware of the others entering. He didn't look around, so he had no idea whether Sybilla was there or not. The monks filed in but he was only conscious of their moving robes, the sounds of their own chants, the flickering candles.

After a while he noticed that he was engulfed in silence. He opened his eyes and saw that the candles had been snuffed and the lights turned off. There was only one dimmed overhead light which allowed him to find his way to the entrance of the empty chapel. He picked up his umbrella and trekked back to the guest house in the rain, practically oblivious to his surroundings.

It was only when he got to his room that he saw her note which had been slipped under the door. It was on lined notepaper. One side had a drawing of a beautiful white innocent-looking unicorn curled up by a fountain, a smile on its lips, a gleam in its eye. It was from one of the tapestries at the Cloisters. On the other side was an invitation. "My place. Nine p.m. B.Y.O.B. S."

I LEFT THE CHAPEL WHEN THE OTHERS DID. He was still there. I hurried back to the guest house to get ready for him. I didn't want to change. I had already done so after our rainy escapade. I did want to doll myself up a bit. Not too much. I brushed my teeth. A little lipstick, a little blush, just the tiniest bit of eyeliner and mascara. The final touch, a little spritz of Sortilege. I didn't want to smell like $50 for all night upstairs. I kicked off my flats. It would be dark. I would see to that. I turned off all of the lights except the small lamp on the desk and faced it backward so it reflected on the wall. Candles. I always traveled with candles. I liked to burn them while I was meditating or taking a bath. I had several flat candles a friend had given me which fit neatly into my carry-on. I pulled out a blue one with, unbelievably, the Virgin Mary on it. How propitious! I set it on the bedside table. Now for the music. I agonized over my choice. It had to be sexy and romantic but also not too intrusive. Also, I wanted to set a dominatrix tone. It was, after all, at my place. I was going to take charge. It was I who would take him tonight. Lucky devil. He wouldn't know what hit him.

I thought about Puccini but that was too serious. Religious choral music? Not exactly the mood I had in mind. Diana Krall, with her sultry voice would be a good choice. No. Too supper club. Then it came to me. Tantric music. In one of my yoga classes the teacher had played it. I had to admit it was terribly sensual, especially the tantric shaman music with drumming. Sadly, I had had nobody I wanted to practice tantric sex with. Certainly not Spraig. If ever there was anyone who was not into the idea of a mystical union, it was he. As for the tantric yoga sessions my instructor had suggested, I demurred. Nevertheless, I remained curious. Tonight, I would satisfy my curiosity, as well as other things.

He knocked on the door. I got up from the bed and opened it. The atmosphere was suddenly charged with sexual electricity. He looked gorgeous. His hair had dried in a tousled mop on his head. He had on a black turtleneck and black jeans. He was barefoot. No socks. He was holding an almost empty bottle of Jameson's. I instinctively backed away. He walked past me into the room, set the bottle down on the desk and perused his surroundings approvingly. He could smell my perfume. The lights were very dim and the candle was burning. The tantric music was thrumming softly in the background. I waited until he turned around. He was standing at the foot of the bed. His eyes were burning through me, but he didn't make a move. He must have intuited that it was my night.

Slowly I walked toward him. He stood still, waiting. When I got to him, I too, was still. I looked at him. Then, quietly and gently, I turned him around and pushed him down on the bed. He didn't take his eyes off of me. I climbed on the bed and straddled him. I began making undulating movements over him, moving my body rhythmically to the music. It didn't take long for him to react. I slid up and down, rubbing myself up against him, eliciting a long intake of breath. His hands lay on the bed beside him. He made no attempt to lift them. I brushed my breasts against him and then lay flat for a moment so we could take in the sound of our hearts beating together. I began to undress him. First, I took off his sweater, he raised his arms to help me. Then I licked him on his chest and down to his midriff. I unzipped his pants and pulled them off as he lifted his legs. Next his shorts. I licked his body again, his legs, his abdomen and back up to his lips. I softly licked them, then his neck and his ears. He let out a deep sigh. My eyes never left his. I pulled my sweater over my head and dropped it to the floor. I unhooked my black lace bra and let that fall. I moved off of him to pull down my pants and then my black lace panties. I had placed several pillows against the headboard. I motioned to him to pull himself up to lean against them. He did as I directed.

When he was settled, I methodically climbed on top of him, his legs outstretched, and straddled him again. This time my legs were spread and tucked under my knees so that I was directly above him. Our eyes were closer to each other than ever, our gazes unfaltering. The drumming seemed to be getting louder as was the cadence of our hearts. I hovered over him, occasionally brushing up against him until I was deeply aroused. He didn't move. Just watched. There came a moment when I couldn't bear the anguish of desire another moment. I settled on him and took him inside of me. Except for an inhalation from both of us, there was no sound. I stayed motionless. He followed suit. How long could we both hold off? How long could we both stay in this position, bodies locked, eyes locked? It was tantalizing, a form of delicious torture. In a meditation posture, our bodies melted into each other. It was beyond physical or emotional. It was a profound sense of intimacy. It was transcendent. I have no idea how long we were like that, mesmerized by each other's gaze, by each other's bodies, by each other's spirits. I don't even remember when we came. All I can remember is blacking out for a moment, feeling as if I had lost myself and found myself in him.

Friday

FITZ HAD COVERED HER UP, turned out the lights and left her asleep. It had been, to say the least, an active day. He had slept soundly that night and woke up at nine, invigorated, looking forward to the day. How could he not? The spirit of magical, mystical temptress Sybilla enshrouded him. She had been so different the night before. She had taken over and he had totally surrendered, a new experience for him in the annals of lovemaking. Without a doubt, the most erotic experience he had ever had. Every time he thought he knew her, knew what to expect, she confounded him. Always in the most fortuitous way. She had an innocence about her, a sort of intellectual blue stocking seriousness which belied the fact that she was, in fact, an insatiable sex addict. He grinned and stretched. What a wonderful way to start the day. Except it was also nearing the end. He had been living in a dream, a fantasy. Soon, he would leave. But first he had a session with Father Joseph at ten. A come-to-Jesus meeting if ever there was one.

When last they met, he had not lain (what an old-fashioned word but it seemed apt) with Sybilla yet. Now his whole world was turned upside down. He was not prepared. He wasn't prepared to tell the truth and he wasn't prepared to lie. The thought crossed his mind that he could always cancel the meeting. Somehow that didn't seem like the right thing. He had to have a reckoning, not only with Father Joseph but more importantly with himself. He could not leave here without it.

He went upstairs to find the others finishing breakfast and preparing to depart. He was surprised. He hadn't expected them to leave until Saturday. He panicked suddenly, wondering if Sybilla would be leaving, too. She wasn't there. Of course, the two of them had never discussed it. They had hardly spoken. He wondered if she knew he was not leaving today. Somehow, he had gotten used to seeing them all. They were part of the *mise-en-scène.* He worried that their leaving would change the dynamics of his relationship with Sybilla. Would it be just the two of them alone at meals, at the services? He couldn't imagine how that would work. What if, now that there was nobody to hide from, the thrill of danger had subsided and she had lost interest in him? He nodded goodbye to the two women and the pudgy man who were loading up their cars. Much to his relief he noticed that The Indian guy, the novitiate, he had decided, was not leaving and had gone back into the dining room to refill his coffee cup. Thank God! He was still here. The intermediary.

Again, he was ravenous. Nothing like breathtaking sex to stimulate the appetite. He loaded up on breakfast. When he got to his seat there was an envelope on the table in front of him. It was addressed to Archbishop Kelly. He opened to find a note.

"Dear Archbishop," it said. "I'm not sure that's the right way to address you. I would like to say that it was an honor to meet you although we never had a chance to meet properly. I will say that it was an honor to be in your presence. I have seen you on TV many times. You should know that I am a huge fan. I have read all of your books and am looking forward to reading your new one. I am a 'lapsed' Catholic, if that is even possible. My husband died several years ago of ALS and, I'm sorry to say, I lost my faith after such a cruel and painful experience. Books were my salvation and yours in particular. I have been struggling so to understand, which is what brought me here. The fact that you are here gave me an enormous lift. Just to know that someone like you is in need of answers too, gives me hope that I may find a path to peace. If you're ever in Boca Grande, Florida, I would be happy to arrange an event for you. I am President of the Book Club at the Gasparilla Inn and we do a lot of these with famous authors. Please let me know. It would be a great pleasure for me to finally have the opportunity to speak with you. You are a fascinating man! Best, Diane (Dee Dee) Hawthorne."

On the envelope it had her address, her email, and her phone number. He sighed and stuck it in his pocket. He would have to reply to her note when he got home. Notes like that were not uncommon for him. He didn't relish getting them. It always made him feel sad for the woman and guilty. He didn't want to hurt anyone's feelings. He wanted nothing more than to reach out to her, to give her some sympathy and encouragement. But over the years he had found that he always had to be careful about leading anyone on. He even had to affect a rather rigid and cold facade so as not to give them the slightest indication that he was in any way available. That was rich. He might as well have been wearing a sign around his neck here that read "I am available." Sybilla had picked up on it. Why not Dee Dee? Was he really putting out sexual vibes? He didn't like it about himself that he was just the tiniest bit disappointed that he didn't get a note from the sour Arianthe. Maybe she wasn't so sour, though. Maybe she was hurting too. She was here after all. Oh, well. You can't have it all. He smiled at the irony of his attempt to make himself unobtainable. He was also a bit disgusted with himself for his rather narcissistic take on the situation. Maybe he was right when he told the pinch-faced Father Schmidt that pride was his downfall. He loved being adored. Fitz was a well-known host in Dublin. His residence was the most sought-after invitation in town. He had dinner parties at least once a month, usually filled with a mix of the local power hierarchy, visiting politicians, diplomats, journalists, writers, entertainers, athletes, and his most gregarious friends. The Taoiseach, the Prime Minister of Ireland was a frequent guest. Maybe he ought to spend a little more time on that flaw rather than mooning over Sybilla.

He got up to get a cup of coffee and went back to his seat. He hadn't expected to see Sybilla, and he was relieved to have a moment alone, especially as it was nearing ten.

As he walked out, he noticed there was an envelope waiting for Sybilla at her place. He suspected it was not from Dee Dee. He stepped into the hall, where the light was soft, and made his way down the corridor.

Father Joseph was waiting for him, a welcoming smile on his face.

"Ah, good morning, Fitz," he said. "I'm happy to see you. Our last meeting and your last day."

"I'll be sorry to leave you, Father. I will be sneaking out at dawn tomorrow. I have an early breakfast with the Vatican Ambassador, a lunch with the Irish Ambassador, and then off to Rome to see the Pope. Back to real life I'm afraid."

"Tell me," said Father Joseph. "What has become clear to you since last we met?"

It seemed like a loaded question.

"In two days?" replied Fitz. And then in what seemed like a rather flippant answer, "That I am one flawed son of a bitch . . . forgive me Father."

"Aren't we all?" he replied. Then added rather quizzically, "But you don't seem terribly depressed about that discovery."

"Well, I'm not really. I've learned that I am human, which of course I've always known but always repressed."

"How so?"

Fitz hadn't expected that question and wasn't exactly sure how to answer it. Not without revealing himself, though that was the whole point of the session. He was already feeling a bit uneasy.

"I mean," continued Father Joseph, "that you seem particularly exuberant for someone who has been agonizing over his flaws. If that is, in fact, what you have been doing."

Fitz couldn't look him in the eye. "For the most part, yes."

"In our last session you told me about Dierdre. I must say, it was one of the most heartbreaking stories I have heard. Does her memory contribute to your acknowledging your flaws?"

"It does, Father. Greatly."

"How so?"

"I felt responsible for her death. I felt I had wronged her, led her into a sinful relationship. I swore to God that I would spend the rest of my life in penance for that in his service. I have tried to do that physically, psychologically, emotionally, even spiritually. But I have not been able to fulfill my pledge. The problem is that I don't know what to do. Yes, I have been praying and meditating and thinking these past five days, but the answers are not coming easily. I have not lost my faith, if that's what you're thinking. But I have lost my belief in the Church as an institution. I don't believe the Church has become what God intended it to be and certainly not what Jesus had in mind. The Church has become a bureaucratic bastion of immorality, exclusiveness, narrow-mindedness, rigidity, and in some cases downright evil. The rot in the Church has superseded the good. It has led to complete anomie. I'm more and more conflicted about being a representative of it when I can't justify so many positions the Church takes."

"How have you dealt with your doubts?"

Fitz pondered the question. It was a hard one.

"I feel that God has put me in this place at this time to do something and that's what I'm trying to do. But it has been met with more and more opposition from the Vatican since my protector and friend, the Pope, died. The new Pope is not a fan."

"You know that?" Father Joseph asked.

Fitz laughed. "He and his minions have made it quite clear, which is why I have been summoned. I feel the Church needs to be more compassionate. It fails in the area of 'brotherly love.' Jesus put community first. Progress and change are anathema. The Church thinks in centuries, not days."

"Hasn't that always been the case?"

"Father, you live the monastic life. It's far removed from the day-to-day life that I live, dealing with real people and real problems. I deeply respect the choice you have made and believe me there are days

I have been sorely tempted to take up the life of silence and solitude. It's just not what I have been called for."

"As you've said."

"Take the child sexual abuse scandal, which I obviously don't need to explain to you. The Church was a closed shop, so inward-looking, so protective of its own, afraid if it spoke openly about it, it would have caused a huge scandal. Well, guess what? It did. I have come under enormous criticism for speaking out. So be it. One evening a priest came to see me. He said, 'I've never seen you so angry in my life.' I had just had a visit from a mother and father. They told me their priest had asked their son to mow his lawn. 'We handed our child over to him,' they said. 'It's not just the children who were abused. It was their families, their futures.' In my sitting room there has been an incredible litany of horrors. People crying like babies. Stories in great detail. Stories of suicide. They didn't believe the victims. I couldn't but react in a way to stop it. Anybody who actually heard those stories couldn't react any other way. I hired one of the best law firms in the country to represent these people. Yet one priest said to me that I was supposed to protect the Church. I told him I had a responsibility to protect the people. The Church would say they had to give the abusing priest another chance. One of the great euphemisms was, 'Father has a little problem,' treating it as if he were an alcoholic or a gambler. An eight-year-old boy told his parents that a priest had asked him to say mass with him. The priest told the boy he had sweets for him and took the child's hand and placed it in his pocket. I went to visit a school and I arrived early so I looked inside a classroom just to see what an eight-year-old boy looked like. How could he have done something like that to someone that size?"

Fitz's voice had begun to quake with rage. "I'm sorry, Father. I'm running on. I just get exercised about this subject and the attitude of 'the,' or rather 'our' Church."

"You owe me no apologies. I'm as outraged by these stories as you are."

"What drives me crazy is that there are so many priests, even now, who are saying it never happened. You say, 'Well something happened.' And they'll say, 'Only once.' Or they'll say they don't remember. They're in denial. In order to abuse a child you have to overcome inbuilt inhibitions. Once that breaks down it becomes compulsive."

"Why do you think other priests are not outraged?"

"They don't want to know. They're just out of touch with reality. One of them told me that I wanted to know too much. Much of the leadership of the Irish Church has its head in the sand. They don't realize how bad the situation is."

"Which is why you wrote *Why Celibacy*?"

This could be getting close to treacherous territory. When Fitz had written *Why Celibacy?* it had never occurred to him that he might, in fact, be close to breaking his vows again. It was not personal. Then. He had to be careful.

"You know, Father, falling in love is a very natural thing. It has happened to many of us. It happened to Thomas Merton. It is not sinful. It is the opposite. There is a sacredness in a sense of commitment and permanence. Unfaithfulness and casual sex are different. But if a priest has an affair, is it a private question? If I fall in love with somebody and become emotionally entangled, if found out and I ditch the woman, that leaves her to carry the burden. If she had a child, that is even more of a cross for her to bear and for me. And ultimately for the Church. Mind you, this happens every day and the Church looks the other way. I see no reason why celibacy couldn't or shouldn't be optional. I certainly would never be against it. In many cases it is, in the Anglican Church and the Orthodox. If a person is celibate and unfaithful to his or her vows, they probably would be unfaithful in marriage as well."

Fitz didn't realize what he was saying until he said it. If he had broken his vows to the Church what would stop him from being unfaithful in marriage? He couldn't ever imagine being unfaithful to Sybilla. But then he couldn't ever have imagined being unfaithful to his vows, certainly not since Dierdre. Now he was in more of a quandary than ever. He would have to continue this conversation with trepidation.

"Of course, there is a value of keeping celibate, if one can demonstrate that they can live their sexual life in a way that shows a faith in the God they serve. There's so much confusion around sexuality today. So many young people in our current culture can't live without sexuality. But honestly, people not becoming priests is not just about celibacy. There are too many priests doing things that priests shouldn't be doing. There are those who say if a priest hasn't changed nappies, they shouldn't be priests. I'm not an expert on marriage but if I could be a witness to the gospel of Christ as a married man, if I could bring a spiritual quality to the priesthood, wouldn't that make me a better priest than those who have abused their office? The Catholic Church is turning young people against faith. We have to create a community that people will want to join. That's what I am trying to do. But the Church is so moralistic. It has so many rules that they prevent people from getting to know Jesus Christ. As Catholics, we grew up being taught that the world is black or white. But we live in a gray area now. Christianity is not the only religion in the world. It's a religion of reaching out a hand to pick you up. We should be quick to help people start again, not abandon them. There is no such thing as an ideal Catholic. That's rubbish. There is never the ideal. There is only the constant challenge." Fitz sat back in his chair and let out a breath. "You didn't expect to hear a sermon today, did you?" he asked Father Joseph.

"You're good," Father Joseph replied. "Very persuasive. I'm impressed. You didn't say anything that I could disagree with. But then, that's not my job."

"Would you define your job as listening to rants from reprobate Archbishops desperately in need of counsel?"

"Reprobate, are we?"

"That's how I see it."

"In need of counsel?"

"Desperately."

"Well then. We're almost at lunch time. I already gave you a second session on Wednesday. How about another one this afternoon? After midday prayer. I think we still have a lot more talking to do. I don't want you to leave here without some sense of perspicuity. Which, I gather, you have not achieved."

"Brilliant deduction, Father," he said. "I'm not sure I'm looking forward to it. But I will be here a little after two-thirty."

Father Joseph smiled as he patted Fitz on the hand before ushering him out the door.

I woke up at ten and thought being able to sleep so late might have been the greatest benefit I had gotten from being at the retreat. At home I always jumped out of bed and went to work, anxious to start the day, deliberately avoiding Spraig who slept in after a late night's work. But then, at home, work was all I had to look forward to. Here I could luxuriate in the knowledge that I had no commitments. I didn't have to talk to anyone, I didn't have to call the super because the sink was leaking or worry about how I was going to get out of a lunch or a book party I really didn't want to go to. I didn't have to think about what to have for dinner or pretend to be asleep when Spraig crawled into bed, sometimes significantly after his show had ended. Here at the monastery I had finally found the peace I was looking for. Not to mention the love. That, however, was an oxymoron. There was certainly no peace in my feelings for Fitz.

I had to admit I was very pleased with my performance last night. He actually had been, pardon the expression, blown away. The fact that I had never done anything like that before, that I learned it all from reading about tantric sex, was even stunning to me. It made me laugh just to remember the look on his face as he was being dominated by me. It had been divine.

But I had no idea where Fitz was now. I had no idea when he was leaving. Of course, he couldn't have discussed his departure with me, we had barely spoken, keeping our vows of silence, but it was the end of the week. What if he were leaving today! Not possible. He would never just walk out on me without at least a goodbye note or an explanation.

On the other hand, if he were truly conflicted, he might well do that. It would be easier. Less painful. At least for him. I started to get out of bed, get dressed and run upstairs to find him. Where, though? I couldn't imagine he would be wandering around. Services were over. It was really raining so I didn't think he had gone out for a walk or a run. I thought about knocking on his door and rejected that idea, then checked the floor by my door to see if there was a note. Nothing. Retreating back into my room, I heard a ping on my phone. It was a text from Spraig.

"WTF?!"

My, he certainly had a way with words. Or letters, as the case may be. At least there were no nasty emojis. Oh, wait! There it was. The grimacing face.

I didn't respond.

My phone started to ring. It was Spraig. I didn't pick up. He called several times. I knew he was swearing at his cell. I waited until he had ceased calling.

I decided to check my email. There was one from Maman. From this morning.

"*Ma chérie, Qu'est-ce qu'il se passe? J'ai parlée ce matin a Spraig. Il est tellement faché avec toi. Il m'a dit que tu refuse de lui parler. Il a demandé que je te telephone. Je m'inquiète. Ça va? Appelles-moi tout de suite, s'il te plait. Je t'adore. Maman.*"

So Spraig had called her and told her he was angry with me because I refused to talk to him. He wanted her to call me. Of course she was worried. But I didn't want to call her right away. I wasn't in the mood.

I wrote back, "*Chére Maman, Je t'adore aussi. Tu sais que je n'ai pas le droit de parler ici. C'est mon dernier jour. Je reviens demain. Je t'appelerai en arrivant chez moi. Grosse Bises. Sybilla.*"

I knew she wouldn't be happy with that. But I was not calling her.

She'd have to wait until tomorrow.

There were too many other emails to even read them. They would have to wait. Only one other required a reply. Duncan.

"My precious girl. Are you having just the most fabulous time? I still can't believe that you are there cloistered with a group of old monks eating fruit cake and not talking. Tell me the truth, have you fallen madly in love with one of them? Are you going to take up the cloth? That's the only excuse for not communicating with me. Anyway, I miss you terribly. What time do you get in tomorrow? Why don't you ditch the husband and have dinner with me? I'm longing to hear every detail. Your devoted admirer. D."

I emailed back immediately.

"I'd love to. Raoul's? xo"

I was almost giddy at the thought of having a long, gossipy, wine-filled dinner with Duncan instead of confronting Spraig. Raoul's had a great tarot card reader, who I found irresistible. Duncan was the only one I had ever talked to about Spraig. He detested Spraig. He thought Spraig was a malignant narcissist. Duncan had been my savior through all of this trauma. I really hadn't wanted to involve Maman and Father. They would worry too much. Duncan had a sense of humor about it and a sense of perspective. I discussed it endlessly with him. He was really my shrink. I knew he would be able to get the truth about Fitz out of me: once we had gotten our tarot cards read and he'd told me we were both destined to fall in love with Catholic priests before laughing and ordering another glass of wine.

As I went to turn off my phone, another email popped up.

"Dear Ms. Sumner," it read. "We are pleased to inform you that you have been accepted as a visiting writer for the MFA Writer's Workshop at the Sorbonne in Paris . . ." I had to sit down. I really didn't think that they would accept me as I had applied so late. I had told nobody about this, not even Duncan. In fact, I had practically succeeded in putting it out of my mind. I had known about the program, but it had never occurred to me to apply for it. I had only begun to think about it before I decided to come to the monastery. I had applied just to see what would happen. I really had no intention of going. It was just that life with Spraig had become so intolerable that I felt the need to get away. I could have just flown over to Paris to visit Mimi but that would have been as aimless as I had been feeling. I needed a purpose. My work at *The New Yorker* and my book were gratifying but my problems with my marriage had distracted me and I didn't feel like I was doing my best work. I would keep writing in Paris. What I needed was to escape the life I was leading, a life in which I felt imprisoned and without agency. I wanted to live a life of meaning. I could not live it in New York. I could not. I had done nothing but question my values for the past few years. Why was I living this life I detested? Why was I living with a man I didn't love and didn't admire? What had made me tolerate the way he had treated me since we learned he was infertile? Why had I allowed myself to be lost? What had happened to my self-respect? All of those questions were questions that had been there subconsciously but until this moment I had tried to repress them. Now I felt liberated. I had not found myself, but I had discovered a way there.

 I responded right away to the letter, accepting the offer. I would move to Paris immediately. I would find a small flat on the left bank near the Cluny Museum. I would teach at the writer's workshop at the Sorbonne, helping young writers. I would spend weekends at L'Arche, outside of Paris, working with the intellectually challenged, a place I had long admired and that my family had supported.

L'Arche. It had been only in the back of my mind. Somewhere to go on the weekends which would give meaning to my life. Now it was as if all of the work and meditation and prayer and, yes, loving I had been doing this week had led me to the realization that I actually had found what I was looking for. I had worked at L'Arche during summer vacations in the French countryside. It had been emotionally draining but terribly satisfying. Nothing I had ever done had given me the sense of fulfillment and satisfaction as I got while working there. Yet, it was not the life I wanted for myself permanently. I wanted to be a writer. It was all I ever really aspired to do. It wasn't that the work I was doing at *The New Yorker* or even on the book wasn't gratifying. It was that I always felt there was something missing in my life. I needed to be of service in some way. I needed, although it may sound corny, nourishment for my soul. L'Arche would be it. I don't know if I would have come to that conclusion if I hadn't come here to the monastery.

I was momentarily elated. Only then did I think of Spraig. He would be distraught. For a time. He would then meet a beautiful and well-to-do divorcee in Southampton with two kids and live the life he wanted. I expected to feel sad, but I didn't. I simply felt relieved. With great deliberation, I slowly reached down and removed my wedding rings from my finger. I wrapped them in a Kleenex and slipped them into a side pocket of my purse. I waved both hands in the air and felt the real possibility that I might actually take flight.

Turning off my phone, I got dressed in jeans and a heavy, bright blue ribbed cashmere pullover. I wasn't going out so I put on some socks and black suede slides and went upstairs to the dining room. It was empty, as I expected. I got a small container of yogurt out of the fridge to tide me over until lunch. I went to sit down when I noticed an envelope on the table at my place.

I was stricken. It was obviously from Fitz. A farewell letter. How could he!? How could he possibly leave without seeing me? And to put a letter on the bloody table! Not even slipping it under my door! I couldn't decide whether I was more angry or more devastated. I was angry at him for being so callous, angry at myself for being had, devastated that he would care so little for me, devastated that I had lost him.

I wanted to take the letter down to my room to read, fearing I would completely dissolve when I read it, but I couldn't wait. It wasn't his usual thick ecru envelope. It was just a plain white drugstore envelope. Strange.

I tore it open.

"Dear Sybilla," it read. "If I may call you that. I have long admired you from afar. Your work in *The New Yorker* is spectacular and I was so happy for you when you won the MacArthur Genius award. I especially loved the piece you did on unicorns. It was so original. It's hard to imagine someone being so beautiful and intelligent and talented at the same time. This week I've had a chance to admire you from close-up. It took all the restraint I had not to talk to you. The idea of being here for five days with you and not being able to have a conversation was too cruel. I came here for the first time this fall because I needed to figure some things out. I majored in English literature at the University of West Virginia and taught English in high school for years. Recently I retired and moved to a small town called Paw Paw on the Cacapon River. God's country. Sadly, I never married, and I came to a point in my life where I needed to figure out what God had in mind for me. It's been a wonderful week. I loved the silence and the solitude. Even though I have plenty of that in the hills it just isn't the same. What inspired me was the fact that there were other seekers here as well. And when I look at people like you and the archbishop, both so talented and successful, it makes me feel that I am not alone. That there are those out there who are questioning just as I am. I leave here invigorated and at peace, mostly because of your presence. I thank you for that. I doubt that you will ever get to Paw Paw, but if you do, here's where to find me. Sincerely, with the greatest admiration, J. Don Clark. jdonpawpaw@gmail.com."

I teared up. What a sweet and thoughtful letter. I was consumed with guilt. How could I have been such a bitch? I was privately ridiculing him when he was here going through all of the same kinds of personal anguish I was. We all were. That's why we were here. To find answers. And to think I dismissed him so casually was reproachable. I don't think I had ever felt so ashamed. Of course I would email him back. Though not today. I would wait until I got home. I would wait until I had time to absorb, not just his letter, but this whole experience.

I went back to my room. No note under the door. Thank you, Jesus! I would have to wait. My anxiety level was off the charts. When I became anxious the one thing that was most calming was thinking about Spetses. My happy place. When I was describing it to Father Joseph I don't think I really got across to him the magic of the island for me. Before I got accepted to the writer's workshop in Paris, I had often fantasized about living there alone and writing in solitude. One of the reasons for coming to the monastery was to see if I couldn't handle that. Of course, it wouldn't have been the same living there year around. I didn't know whether the winters would have changed my feeling about it. I doubted that though. I realized that Spetses was just a short flight from Paris and my heart leapt up.

I turned on my phone and looked at all of the pictures from this summer and summers past. Late mornings under the pergola or on the balcony off of the kitchen overlooking the sea with fresh bread and homemade honey, fresh figs from our trees, fresh peaches and Greek yogurt, hardboiled eggs and coffee. There was Katerina's beloved kaiki which we took out most days around noon, cruising around the island, stopping at various coves and swimming off the boat. Sometimes we would take a picnic, hunt for sea nettles and split them open, sucking out the delicious insides and drinking much too much Greek wine. Other days, we stopped at a little taverna on the other side of the island and we would eat Greek salad and grilled calamari. Other days we'd come back for a long lunch and a siesta under our canopy and a swim off the rocks.

One of my favorite things to do was ride a Vespa up to the top of the mountain where the pine forests were thickest. It was much cooler up there, the summer breezes were exquisite as were the views from every angle. There were times when I felt totally disassociated from the world, a feeling I grew to like more and more as my world seemed to be disintegrating.

I especially loved the amphitheater at the edge of our property overlooking the sea. There, cocktail hour was sacrosanct—the violet hour, as historian Bernard DeVoto called it. I actually needlepointed a pillow with his words: "This is the violet hour, the hour of hush and wonder, when the affections glow and valor is reborn, when the shadows deepen along the edge of the forest and we believe that, if we watch carefully, at any moment we may see the unicorn."

The sun would be setting in a glorious fusion of reds and pinks and oranges. We would pour our rosé and exclaim how it matched the sky and take pictures of ourselves, raising our glasses in homage to such beauty, such magic. The moon would soon come sliding up from behind the hills, all shimmery and incandescent.

It was an idyllic and indolent summer, full of laughter and fun and pleasure and pure happiness. I stayed the whole month of August, mostly without Spraig, who would show up for maybe a week.

My favorite thing about being in Spetses, my little secret pleasure, was right next door. Our family chapel on the edge of the cliff overhanging the sea. It was a lovely little gem, painted a beautiful Greek blue which stood out as one sailed by it. Inside was an altar, frescos and icons, a few antique chairs and candles. More and more each year I would go there to meditate, to contemplate, maybe even to pray. I found solace and comfort there and it grounded me. It was a sacred space.

Now I began daydreaming about a life with Fitz. I allowed myself to fantasize what it would be like. He would obviously have to quit the Church. I know. That would be a big deal, but it was clear from his writings that he has been disgusted and frustrated by so many aspects of the Catholic Church. Maybe he would come to realize that he could do so much more good from the outside than from the inside. After all, the Church has curtailed so much of his efforts for reform. I imagined the two of us living year-round in Spetses. I wondered if Fitz would like it there. How could he not? Though it was very different from Dublin. My greatest fear was that no matter where we lived, he would ultimately resent me if he left the Church. My second greatest fear was that he wouldn't like Spetses. Of course, I could always write there. But what would he do? We would always be able to take a break every few months. We could go visit my parents, and my grandmother, and spend time in Ireland. No matter where we lived, he could continue to write and speak out against the problems with the Church. Although without his position in the Church he would be giving up his status, his power, his pulpit, and, in many ways, his reputation. He wouldn't even have a sinecure. How would he be able to support himself? Us? Our family? I had some money, but I wasn't rich. If we stayed in my grandmother's house we would be able to live fairly well but it wouldn't be ours. In Dublin he had the archbishop's residence, the staff, the drivers, the connections, the honors, the travel, meetings with the Pope, the prime ministers, the powerful who came to visit and other world leaders at conferences all over the world. He also had the respect of the entire religious community, not just in Ireland but globally. He was a rock star. He also had his faith. He was, in fact, married. It would be worse than ugly. It would be a scandal. How could he be in a relationship with me and with God at the same time?

On the other hand, I rationalized, he would be in a human relationship, a love relationship which he could and never would get from the Church. We might even be able to have children. He could have a family. What a fabulous father he would be. He was the most passionate man I had ever met. If he put his passion toward reforming the Church, toward me, toward our children, wouldn't he, couldn't he be satisfied by that? It was asking a lot. It was asking too much. He would never do it. In the end I didn't really believe he would give up so much.

I would be giving up nothing. I had already decided to leave Spraig. One thing this week that had been made clear was that we had no marriage left. If I got no clarity about anything else, at least I had clarity on that. The idea of divorcing him was difficult but the prospect of living the rest of my life with him was untenable. I had come here to the monastery for answers and that is what I had gotten. I was more in love with Fitz than I could ever imagine possible. The thought of losing him was more than I could bear. But I would lose him. He would not choose me over God. Even though we hardly spoken to each other I knew it in the depths of my being.

I was too distraught to cry. I lay on the bed and let my mind drift back to Spetses and the little chapel. Even though I had the chapels here, both the monks' chapel and the private chapel in the guest house right next to my room, even though I was able to beseech God or the universe or whomever here, I felt as if I needed to be there, in Greece, right now. I remembered my grandmother telling me about an attractive Irish priest who came to Spetses every June from Dublin. They had gotten to know him through Father Christopoulous, the local Orthodox priest. The Irishman stayed at the church in their guest rooms for visiting clergy. It was right on a hill in the Old Port, just above the sea. He had brought the Irishman to meet them and thereafter the Irishman began to come regularly every morning to pray in our chapel, getting the key from the kitchen staff. Finally, Mimi had instructed them to give him a key. He would stop off in the beginning of June each year to greet everyone, never in his cassock, always in shorts and a polo shirt, then quietly go off to the chapel for an hour or so. Once they had invited him and Pater Christopoulos for dinner and the priest had brought his guitar and sang. They were all impressed at how good he was. At the end of June he would send a case of their favorite wine in thanks. I had never really given it much thought although they had mentioned him several times. Now I wondered who he was, what he was doing there. I wondered if Fitz knew him.

On a whim, I sent a second email to my mother.

"*Maman*," I wrote. "*Tu connais le pretre Irlandais a Spetses qui vient chaque jour pendant le mois de Juin pour prier dans notre chapelle? Est-ce que tu sais son nom?*"

I wondered if she would remember him or his name. She wasn't there often in June, but she did go over occasionally to see her mother before we took up residence in August.

"*Oui, bien sur,*" she wrote back immediately. "*Ce n'est pas possible d'oublier cet homme. Il est tres charmant et tres, tres beau—a mourir beau! Dommage qu'il soit pretre! Quel gaspillage! Son nom, je crois, est Kelly. James Kelly. Pourquoi? Je t'embrasse.*"

She was right. It was a shame. It was a terrible waste. *Mon Dieu*!

"*C'est rien. J'ai entendu parler de Kelly et je me souvenais qu'il y avait quelqu'un comme lui á Spetses. Rien d'important. Je t'appelles demain.* xo"

The lunch bell was ringing. I couldn't get upstairs fast enough. I had to see him. He wasn't there. Krish had just arrived and was getting his plate. All of the name tags at the seats were gone except for three. There were only three plates out. Mine, Krish's, and—yes! Fitz's. He wasn't gone. I wasn't all that hungry, but I helped myself to some pot roast, parsley potatoes, and green beans. I didn't want to hurt the cook's feelings. I'd have to see about the fruit cobbler. I poured myself some water and sat down, concentrating on my food and trying not to stare at the door. I took one bite and was barely able to swallow. I was so tense my foot began to shake. Krish got up for some dessert. I was ready to leave when Fitz came in.

Something was different. I could tell immediately by his demeanor. He seemed pensive, distracted. He had seen me when he got to the door but made no attempt to acknowledge my presence. He took his plate, selected very small portions and went to his seat. I noticed out of the corner of my eye that he was playing around with his food but wasn't particularly interested in it. I decided to get some dessert, mainly to see if he would glance over at me. I sat down and pretended to eat. Krish was taking his last bite of fruit cobbler. Oddly, I didn't want to be left alone with Fitz. I was afraid he might say something I didn't want to hear. As soon as Krish got up to wash his dishes, I followed him and quickly went back to my room.

I sat on the edge of the bed in a state. What had happened between now and last night? I would have expected him to be ebullient. I was ebullient. And excited about my decision to go to Paris. I wanted more than anything to be able to tell him about it. He gave no sign of elation, rather he seemed dejected. I heard him come back to his room and shut the door. I tried to read some of the spiritual handouts for a bit, but I couldn't concentrate. Finally, I decided to go up to the chapel early for midday prayer. It would be awkward running into him in the hallway.

By now it was pouring rain and despite my umbrella and jacket I was pretty well soaked. I sat down, crossed myself, and knelt. Whatever it took. He and Krish came in together. He didn't even look my way but went right to his seat, genuflecting, crossing himself, kneeling. I could only see the back of his head. The whole thing was a blur. I should have been praying or something, but nothing came into my mind but, "Please God." My new mantra. It seemed like forever but, mercifully, the service finally ended. I leapt up, got my umbrella and dashed down to the guest house. There was no note under the door. I didn't know whether that was a good sign or a bad sign. Didn't know anything anymore. All I knew was that what was happening was not propitious. I undressed, took a long hot shower, washed my hair, and climbed into bed. Now what was I going to do with myself for the rest of the afternoon? I almost called Duncan and then thought better of it. I didn't want to have that conversion over the phone, and I wasn't ready to tell him about the Sorbonne.

Besides, I didn't know what to say. I would have to wait. Again. Then it occurred to me that I still didn't know when Fitz was leaving. Could it be this afternoon? There wasn't really much for him to do if he couldn't go for a walk or a run. He probably was all prayed out. Perhaps he was also all played out. If true, that was too painful for me to even contemplate.

I couldn't stand it a minute longer. I had to get out of there. But where? It was raining too hard to go for a walk, but the claustrophobia was making me crazy. I still did not believe he would just leave without a word. It was unthinkable that I wouldn't see him again. If we did see each other, our last night together, it was bound to be fraught. It occurred to me then that we had drunk the last of the Jameson. Whatever might happen that night we were going to have to be lubricated. At least I was.

I googled the closest liquor store: ABC Liquor in Berryville, a seventeen-minute drive away. I jumped off the bed, picked up my bag and dashed up the stairs, car keys jangling in my hand. I grabbed an umbrella from the hall and ran out to the car, my shoes filling with water. The rain was coming down so steadily that I needed my brights and even with them I could barely make out the definition of the road. I turned on the heater, turned off the music I'd been listening to when I'd driven down to the retreat, and had my windshield wipers going full blast. Even so, I had to pull over on the side of VA Route 7 West, so blinding was the torrent. I don't know why I felt so desperate to get there. In my mind it seemed that everything hung on whether or not I could obtain that bottle of booze.

When the rain slackened, I started up again and headed into town, past the Veramar Vineyard. The Nalls Farm market was already displaying vast orange and white pumpkins, a sign that fall was really upon us. Berryville, with the Blue Ridge Mountains in the distance, was quaint and tiny so I wasn't worried about finding the ABC store. I drove by the Clarke County Historical Association, a small two-story house with a large curved front porch perfect for sitting in a rocking chair and drinking sweet tea, watching the neighbors stroll by. I came to the Circle K gas station and turned onto Crow St. There it was. Since it was still pouring I got out of the car with my umbrella and made it to the front of the liquor store more or less dry. It was Friday afternoon and quite busy but the nice young woman at the counter couldn't have been more helpful. I asked for a bottle of Jameson. She wasn't sure they had any, but she left her position to go look for me. She came back beaming and exclaimed in triumph, "We had one bottle!" I practically hugged her. Optimism overcame me and I realized I was starving. She sent me across the street to Camino Real Mexican Restaurant which was also beginning to fill up as the locals started getting off of work. I found a table in the back of the cozy well-lit room and immediately ordered a margarita—I would save the hard stuff for later—and a combo platter, one taco, one enchilada and one tamale for $13.00. The waitress was welcoming and even called me "honey." I'm sure she was curious why I was alone on a Friday afternoon and wanted to know if I was "from around these parts." I told her I was staying at the monastery. "Oh wow!" she said. She gave me a look of sympathy as if she knew the pain I had been going through. I felt comforted. It wasn't until I had the exchange with her that I realized I was speaking to someone other than Father Joseph for the first time in five days. It seemed strange, disorienting.

I couldn't remember the last time I had eaten Mexican food. Even though I was from Boston I had developed a liking for it in college. Spraig hated it and refused to go with me, even when I had a craving. I wondered if Fitz liked it or whether he had ever had it before. There was so much that I didn't know about him, that we didn't know about each other. Maybe tonight we might learn more.

I lifted my glass to myself, to my new life, and took a rather large gulp. Nothing had ever tasted so delicious. Up went my glass again. To Spraig. "Fuck you!" I whispered. Another gulp. To Fitz. "To us!"

I ordered another margarita and devoured my meal.

***

THE FIRST SESSION WITH Father Joseph had left Fitz feeling unmoored, caught between two worlds. He felt cut off from what he considered leaving behind but not connected to the possibility of a new future. His anger at the Church had come out in the meeting but so had his passion and concern. And love. He was in more of a conundrum now, on his last day, than he was when he arrived. That first day he had been confident and strong, more exhausted and frustrated than spiritually depleted. Now he was those things as well as incredulous and elated, not to mention besotted. He did not know what to do. He could sense Sybilla's confusion and hurt. He knew he should have written her a note, but he didn't have time this morning before he went to see Father Joseph and then afterward, well, afterward he had become completely disoriented.

Lunch had been miserable. He'd barely eaten. She'd gotten up and left as soon as the Indian guy did, obviously not wanting to be left alone with him any more than he did with her. He tried to write her a note when he got back to his room. He had no words. He heard her leave early for midday prayer. He needed to pray as well so against his better judgment he went too. He tried to summon God in the chapel but he was nowhere to be found. He could have sworn he heard a voice saying, "You're on your own kid!" He was anguished. She'd left before he could even stand up. She must have run back because she disappeared so quickly. It was pouring and he covered his head with his hood and pulled out the umbrella. He barely had time to change out of his wet boots before his next session with Father Joseph. He would have to wait until that was over before he tried to write to her again. He hated himself. He hated what he was doing to her. He hated . . . no. He didn't hate God, but he did not understand what God was doing. He wanted—needed—answers. He wasn't getting them from above. He prayed that Father Joseph could help him.

Fitz walked into the room. Before Father Joseph could rise to greet him, he sat down.

"Let's cut to the chase, Father," he said. "I'm in the bardo. I don't want to leave here in this state." He slammed the table with both hands. "I can't leave here in this state."

"You're certainly not as exuberant as you were when you came here this morning."

"I'm not sure I need an intellectual conversation, or even a spiritual one," Fitz said. "I think I need psychological direction. I need a shrink."

"Actually, what you need," said Father Joseph, "is a psychospiritual form of religion. What does psychology have to tell us about our spiritual life? There has to be a balance of the two. You mention the bardo. Thomas Merton believed in a connection with the Asian tradition. Most American Catholics have kept away from mysticism. It's held in great suspicion by your favorite place, the Vatican. But you can't get away from the intellectual either. Today, deep thinking is suspect. Most seminarians have dropped this. Merton was interested in existentialism. People don't ask those questions anymore. That's why there are so few monks now. Younger people are no longer followers of Merton. They're not really spiritual seekers. They want rules and regulations. They're administrators. I've actually had a priest say to me, 'I'm not a spiritual man.' To be a monk serves no function. It's a vocation to obedience, a community to serve God. It's our way of proclaiming the Gospel. Unless you're interested in spiritual development, you're not going to find it a satisfying life."

Fitz felt impatient with Father Joseph for the first time. He was not cutting to the chase. He seemed to be rambling on. Fitz wasn't interested in being a monk. Far from it. He was interested in changing his life. The problem was, he didn't know exactly how. Or to what.

"Father." His tone was short. "You know the life of solitude does not interest me. I need spiritual direction."

"You know, Fitz, I strongly advise you to read *Mystical Journey: An Autobiography*. It's by your fellow countryman William Johnston, a Jesuit priest. He moved to Japan, discovered Zen Buddhism and it transformed the way he thought about Christian mysticism. He was also a friend of Merton's. He believed in meditation and contemplation, as well as prayer."

"I do know William Johnston," Fitz said. "But I don't want to talk about him right now."

"I have an extra copy. It could be the perfect book to read on your flight to Rome. Given what you're facing, you will need to be in a zen mode."

"I'm going to need more than that, I'm afraid."

"You talk about wanting a shrink. You know Buddhism has been practicing psychoanalysis for centuries. They are much more preoccupied with the self than we Christians are. We're more focused on Christ and God and the Holy Trinity."

"What's the difference between psychoanalysis and spiritual direction?"

"Spiritual direction is to listen but also to re-verbalize. It's the process of helping someone reconnect. It allows you to question things you've repressed or denied, but it is not to be feared. The director doesn't have the answers. His job is to accompany people through the natural process, to give them the feeling that they have been listened to, that they are not alone, that they are not the first person this has happened to. We give permission to do things differently because things have failed before. You don't have to keep doing it. I call it spiritual accompaniment, not 'direction.' We help each other."

"Then how does praying still make sense?"

"I studied Freudian psychology. Why am I still doing petitionary prayer? There's a complex answer. We are living in a state where God is infinitely remote. Being intimate with God is more about being intimate with myself. I am not in a state of alienation. God is the ground of my being. If I meet my true self, I will meet God there."

"I don't understand."

"What I'm trying to say is that our culture does not take metaphor seriously. From psychology we know the importance of myth. I'm not taking myth literally. I only use myth to describe reality that cannot be described any other way. Myth has to be expressed. Symbolism too. Sadly, our culture does not recognize that."

Fitz was shaken. He couldn't believe what Father Joseph had just said.

"Are you saying that you don't really believe in God? You believe that 'God' is a myth? 'God' is symbolic? Is that what you mean?"

"That's a bit simplistic, I'm afraid. What I'm saying is that God is what we need him to be. God is not anthropomorphic. We can't become God. Nor can God become us. We can aspire to be in the image of what or whom we wish God to be at any given time. Greek mythology is a perfect example of that."

"Okay. So, if you are accompanying me spiritually and we are helping each other, what do we say to one another?"

"I would tell you to trust in your God, if that's how you want to refer to the guiding spirit within you. But more importantly, if you believe that God made you in his image, you must believe in yourself. You must believe in the goodness of God and your own goodness."

"I just told you I was deeply flawed. How can I trust in my own goodness?"

"You are a good person Fitz. You are a Godly person. And that goodness will show you the way."

Fitz stood to pace up and down the room as he stared out at the rain. He ran his fingers through his hair, sat down, and said, "Father. There is something I must confess to you."

"I'm not your confessor."

"Father. I've met someone," Fitz said.

"Yes," said Father Joseph. "She's very beautiful. Inside and out."

"You know." It was a statement. Not a question.

The monk nodded.

Fitz buried his face in his hands. "Oh God, Father. I don't know what to do."

"I can't help you, dear boy," he said gently. "It's you who must decide."

"I'm so afraid. Not for myself. For her. At the beginning of this week I thought it might be God's will. That he had sent us here to be together. But now I don't know. I love God, or whoever I believe God to be. I love Sybilla. I will always love them both. I want to serve God, to serve good, for the rest of my life. I also want to love in a fully human way. Must I choose between them?"

"You know," said Father Joseph, "I will have to defer to the master, Thomas Merton. 'We must make the choices that enable us to fulfill the deepest capacities of our real selves.' Fitz, you have to put fear aside. You cannot make this decision out of fear. You must have the courage of your convictions."

"That's my problem, Father. I'm just not sure what my convictions are right now. I told you I was a flawed human being. Never so flawed as at this moment. I came here for a reason: to find myself. And, unfortunately, I've been successful. My epiphany has been that I've been selfish, hypocritical, and narcissistic. The truth is, that I really love being the archbishop. I love the adulation, I love the attention, I love the publicity, I love the power, I love being a player."

"Your epiphany?"

"Father Schmidt helped me along." Father Joseph smiled sadly, shaking his head. "But I really do detest the institution. I've tried to rationalize to myself that I can do more good from within than from without on the issues of sexual abuse, women priests, homosexuality, and celibacy, but that's not good enough. It's a lot to give up. And I don't know what I would do with the rest of my life. I don't know if there's a way that I can make more of an impact. But I do know what I want. I want to be with Sybilla. I want to love her. I want to marry her. I want to father her children. Yet I don't know if I have the courage to leave. I'm not sure I do. I've tried to pray to God, to ask him to help me decide. I've gotten no response at all. I feel more heard by you, more understood by you than I do by God."

"Ah, finally we're making progress."

Father Joseph paused.

"Your honesty is beautiful. Yes, you are egotistical. People who make great strides in their spiritual life are those who are looking at their deeper self and see it starting to emerge. Every real spiritual person is humble because they have seen themselves."

Fitz didn't respond.

"You have had a call to reflection through silence. What have you observed here while examining your soul?"

Again Fitz said nothing. He seemed lost in thought.

"Fitz, is there anything you do love about what you do besides the adulation, the attention, the celebrity, the power? Do I sound like Father Schmidt?"

Fitz looked stunned. He closed his eyes and began shaking his head. He put his hands over his eyes and ran his hands through his hair.

"Oh my God, Father."

"Do I sense a bit of humility coming on?"

"I love my work, Father. I love God, I love Jesus. I believe in the real presence of them in the Eucharist. Every day I wake up and thank God for being able to live a life of service to him, to others. I hear confession, I christen babies, I marry people, I care for the sick, I give last rites, I bury the dead. I get out of bed at three a.m. many mornings to go to someone in need. They come to me with their problems, with their anguish. I believe I can help them. I can give them a sense of dignity. That is the greatest gift anyone can have. I can't imagine ever doing anything more rewarding in my life. I will never not do that. I'm sorry if I have given you the impression that this is not why I stay. It is why I stay. I believe that my rage at the Church is fired by my love of the church."

"Have you ever considered leaving the Catholic Church? You know, as an Anglican priest you could marry and have children."

Surprise, offense, then shame flitted across Fitz's reddening face.

"Aye, I have thought about it," he admitted. "But I just as quickly dismissed the idea. I could no more do that than give up my Irish passport for a British one. I have little patience with these guys who think they can have it all. I was born a Catholic, I will die a Catholic. It's unthinkable."

"It was just an idea," said Father Joseph.

He hesitated for a moment, then looked directly at Fitz.

"God's love is always present. You can never lose it. But it only comes in silence."

He let that sit for a minute.

"You know, all the things you are asking of God you already have.

You have God's love, as does Sybilla. She represents God's love and she awakens in you a sense of your own happiness. No matter what happens, you both need to leave here knowing you will be fine."

"But I have so many questions. I guess I'm searching for a sign."

"God doesn't answer questions. You have to follow your heart and your passion, whatever they may be. All you need to do is to ask what the silence has taught you."

"Be still and know that I am God."

"I have nothing more to offer you," said Father Joseph, nodding in sympathy. "Except to say that I know you will find the right answers. I have never been more convinced of anything. You know, there is a Japanese art of *Kintsugi*, putting broken pieces of pottery back together with gold. It's really a metaphor for accepting our flaws and healing so that we are stronger and more beautiful than ever. God can put the pieces of your heart back together, Fitz."

He folded his hands and put them on the table in front of him. Fitz had never felt so heard and so alone at the same time. Neither one of them made a motion to stand up.

"I will quote Merton again," said Father Joseph. "It's the advice he gave to me and to many others of us who decided to dedicate our lives to Christ. It may not be what you want to hear but it's the best counsel ever given to me." Fitz waited. "A life is either all spiritual or not spiritual at all. No man can serve two masters. Your life is shaped by the end you live for. You are made in the image of what you desire."

He stood up then. So did Fitz. Father Joseph came around the table and reached out to Fitz, taking him in his strong arms and hugging him until the breath nearly came out of him. Fitz felt as if he were being embraced by his own father, the kind of embrace he had always longed for.

"I will pray for you," said Father Joseph. It was a benediction.

Fitz turned and left quickly before he broke down.

He had to get out of there. It was almost five and darkness was descending. He ran downstairs and changed back into his wet clothes and his running shoes. He put on his windbreaker with the hood. He went upstairs and out the door, not bothering to take an umbrella. He had to run. He could barely see anything it was coming down so hard. He passed the outdoor chapel, the turnoff to the barn and the river and kept going. Soon he was out on the main road and heading right as fast as he could go. The road was empty. It was barren and desolate, just like he felt. His mind was a blank. He didn't want to think or feel anything. He just wanted the punishing rain to blast his body as he tore down the pavement. Occasionally a car with its brights would pass slowly by, one or two even honked as if to offer help. He waved them away and kept on going. He was gasping in water. His lungs felt as if they were filling up and his eyes were so full of liquid that he really couldn't see anything. He was running for his life, as if he were being chased by the devil and was in danger of being caught if he slowed his pace even a little. He had no idea how fast he was going, how far, or where. All he knew was that he could not stop.

After an hour he got to an old farm. His ribs were hurting and he felt his lungs were about to explode. He bent over as if to expel the rain which had engulfed his body. It was dark by now. His breathing was painful. He knew he had to turn back. He could barely see the road. It had to have been miles. Reluctantly he turned around and made his way back to the monastery, still running, though not nearly as quickly as before. He forced himself to keep going until he saw the lights from the retreat house at the top of the hill. He loped slowly back, only then realizing that the rain had stopped. He was totally drenched and chilled to the bone.

Once in his room, he showered, washed his hair, put on his black undershorts and a black T-shirt and lay down on his bed, clasping his St. Christopher's medal. He was still cold from his run. He heard the dinner bell ring. He heard her door open and close. He didn't move. He didn't want to run into Sybilla in this state. He also wasn't hungry. Besides, he had one more thing to do.

He had made his decision. Somehow, on his run, his mind completely emptied and the answers he had been searching for came to him. He had had an epiphany in every sense of the word. Not only was he imbued with insight and clarity, he also beheld the manifestation of Christ in his life. He was so overcome with relief that he lay immobile on his bed. He knew what he had to do.

He arose, went to his desk, and pulled out his stationary. He had to write her a letter.

"My dearest Sybilla."

He was paralyzed. How could he say this? How could he do this?

"This is a letter I never expected to write, never wanted to write. It is a letter I have to write only because what I have come to feel for you these past few days was something I never expected to feel.

"I cherish you in a way I have never cherished anyone or anything in my life, even my God. This is why I must let you go. When I do, you will walk away with my heart and my soul and leave me an empty vessel. Yet I will still have the knowledge that I have given you everything I can at this moment. That, at least, will bring me joy. I have nothing left to give to you, to offer you. I cannot give you a life, certainly not the life you long for and the life you deserve. I am committed to the Church and to my vows and for my sins I must keep those commitments.

"Never doubt that I have not taken this decision lightly. I have agonized over it every minute and every hour since I first laid eyes on you this week. Until this moment clarity has eluded me. What made me see the right path was my deepest and most unconditional love for you and my desire to do what's best for you, for your happiness. I have no doubt that this will be very painful for you. I can only hope that your pain can never compare to the agony I have experienced, am experiencing, and will experience for the rest of my life. Still, my lamentations will be worth the blessing of having known you and loved you. You will be in my dreams for eternity.

"I have spread my dreams under your feet;

"Tread softly because you tread on my dreams. F."

He had to push the letter away to keep his tears from smearing on the page.

Once he finished writing, he lay in bed, listening for her to return. Finally, she came back to her room. He thought perhaps she might slip a note under his door but there was nothing. He started to pack. He had to do something to distract himself. He had hung his cassock in the closet when he first got there. He would put on his collar before he left as he was going directly to the Vatican Embassy. He got out his suitcase and began throwing his clothes in. Father Joseph had left a manila envelope for him at his door. No note. Just a copy of *Mystical Journey: An Autobiography* by the Irish priest William Johnston. He began thumbing through the book and checked out some of the reviews. He was amazed that he hadn't really followed him. So much of the mysticism that Johnston wrote about was reminiscent of Yeats's view of religion. He admired his syncretic attitude toward belief. He was amused that Johnston was a horny bastard, pining after the nuns. He was fascinated by Johnstons's description of "vertical meditation," going down down down to the "center of the soul." He was touched by Johnston's admiration of St. John of the Cross, a Spanish converso who famously preached that "in the twilight of life, God will not judge us on our earthly possessions and human success, but rather on how much we have loved."

That gave him pause. There it was again. The "L" word. It was always all about love. Except it wasn't. Not the kind of love he had discovered. Or was it?

He heard Sybilla's door open and close. She was obviously going to Compline. He had planned to go himself but decided then that he couldn't. There were no prayers left in him. He had nothing to say to God. God was not getting a "Dear John" letter. He would deal with him later.

This would be the time to put the note under her door. He had no idea how she would react. Would she fall apart? Would she ignore it, not reply and just let him leave? Would she respond with a note? Would she come knocking on his door? He couldn't decide which would be worse. On some level he hoped she wouldn't answer and just let him leave. It would be easier that way. He couldn't stand the idea of seeing her again, knowing it would be their last time. On the other hand, he couldn't stand the idea of not seeing her again. For the same reason.

He folded the note and, not bothering to dress, walked across the hall and placed it under her door. For a minute he was tempted to take it back but that would only postpone the agony. As he turned to go back to his room, he saw the candles burning in the chapel next door, the chapel where he had found her crying on the floor and had held her for the first time. Without thinking, he opened the door and entered. Of course he was alone. He felt enormous relief. He needed to be alone in a sacred space, to be alone with his thoughts. He walked up to the altar and instead of bowing, genuflecting, or crossing himself, he sat down on the floor, his legs crossed. He closed his eyes and began breathing, slowly, rhythmically. Down, down, down he went. Until he could go no farther. And what did he find at the "center of his soul"?

He found Sybilla.

I WAS A LITTLE BUZZED on margaritas when I got back and didn't feel like staying in my room so I went up to the library on the main floor and stayed there for a while perusing the religion books on the shelves. I found the space very soothing. The carpeted room, painted in a pale beige and gray with standing bookcases, held only a simple square table with four wooden chairs and of course, a box of Kleenex. Off the reading room was a closed-in porch with picture windows overlooking the meadows and the farmland. I spent a couple minutes taking in the view through the rain, my eyes lingering on the pastures.

I went back to my room, where I tried to read. But one ear was focused on any sounds of movement from across the hall. At dinner, I hurried to the dining room, but he wasn't there. Once again they had put out three plates. Krish and I sat there alone, ignoring each other, listening to Gregorian chants and picking at our Kielbasa and noodles, tossed salad, and applesauce, none of which I ate. It was surreal. After the meal I hurried down the stairs to my room, hoping and dreading a note under the door. Nothing. Where was he? What was going on? His behavior was shocking and indefensible. One thing was certain. He would be at Compline. He surely wouldn't miss the last service of the week, especially that one.

I wanted to get there early and stake out my position. He would have to pass me going in and coming out. I decided I would get up at the end and wait for him to go by me, then join him on our silent walk back to the guest house. As I walked down the hall I saw a light under his door. If he had left, his door would be open. Unoccupied rooms always had open doors.

The rain had stopped but it was still very wet and dark outside. I was thankful for my flashlight. I got to the chapel early. It was empty. I had taken my cell with me for the first time. No praying for me tonight. I needed to be distracted. I began looking at my pictures of Spetses. That usually put me in a good mood but it wasn't working. I finally decided to look at more of my emails from the week. There were hundreds. I went through them in a semi state of disorientation as I found myself being pulled back into my life. The life I no longer wanted.

When I heard Krish coming in I guiltily hid my phone in my jacket pocket but took it out as soon as he was seated in the middle on the right. Still no Fitz. The lights were dimmed. The monks entered. The candles flickered. The chanting began. I took out my phone and started scrolling. Heretical. I couldn't decide which was more depressing, reading my unwanted emails or waiting for Fitz.

Waiting for Fitz? What was I thinking? As if Fitz were the answer to my problems. All these years I had been waiting. Waiting for Spraig to come around. To be the husband I wanted and needed him to be. Waiting to get pregnant. Now waiting for Fitz . . . to what? To complete my life? No! I was the one who had to complete my life. I couldn't depend on anyone else, much less a man, to be the answer to my prayers. I had to make my own life. I had to become the person I wanted to be, the person I knew I could be, and I had to do it alone. Only then would I be able to love and be loved fully. I had instinctively known this when I applied to the Sorbonne although I hadn't thought it through. I had known this too when I realized that I wanted to work at L'Arche, that I wanted to dedicate my life at this time to something larger than myself. I was sick of the person I was. I was sick of her dependency, her despondency, her preoccupation with herself and her needs and wants and depressions. I needed to abandon her and embrace my new self. If Fitz and I worked out that would be fantastic. But if we didn't, I would go on and live my life and learn to be happy. Thank you God for this epiphany! So, I was praying after all.

The minute Compline was over I was out of there, running down the hill, nearly falling several times and out of breath when I arrived back at the guest house. I opened the door to my room. There it was, lying on the floor, a rebuke to my very existence. I flinched. "Stay calm, stay calm," I told myself. I took off my damp jacket and hung it on the back of my chair. I took off my muddy shoes and put them under the window heater to dry. I picked up the letter and cautiously walked over to the bed. I propped up two pillows and lay down to read it. I opened it with trepidation. I already knew what he would say.

"My dearest Sybilla," he began.

My eyes swept down the page. "This is why I must let you go."

I just wasn't prepared for my reaction. I felt as if my insides were falling out. I had trouble absorbing his words. I was crushed. But at the same time, I knew what I had to do. I would have to summon all of my powers of sorcery, seduction, persuasion, and pure cunning to get him to change his mind. But I was determined, and I believed I could do it. I was Delilah. He was Samson. He didn't stand a chance.

I went into the bathroom to begin my magic. I rolled up my hair. I put on a subtle foundation, a little soft gray eyeliner and an even softer eyeshadow. I curled my eyelashes and touched them up with mascara. I brushed on some blusher, dabbed a little powder under my eyes and put on a darker pink lipstick than usual. An oily gloss made my lips shine. I brushed out my hair and teased it a bit to give it some bounce. The lavender lace bra and matching panties were perfect. I had thrown all my old schoolgirl underwear away après Spraig; I knew it was ridiculous to have brought such beautiful lingerie to a silent retreat, but I was glad I had. The white collared cashmere sweater with a fetching zipper. I slipped on my white cashmere socks. Black yoga pants. No shoes. The whole room smelled like Sortilege after I had finished spraying myself—like a million bucks for all night upstairs. I took my bag and stuffed in my flat candles, my cell for music and, last but not least, my bottle of Jameson. I touched my evil eye necklace for good luck.

I was ready. Lookout James Fitzmaurice-Kelly. Here comes Sybilla.

I pulled myself to my greatest height, squared my shoulders, stuck out my breasts, took his letter and headed across the hall. I didn't wait for him to say "come in" when I knocked. I just pushed open the door, stomped in and waved the letter at him.

He was lying on the bed in his underwear, reading. Reading? How could he be calmly reading when our lives were shambolic? La Bohème was playing in the background. A tragic ending for the lovers.

Not a good sign.

He sat up startled, a look of disbelief on his face.

"*C'est quoi cette connerie?*" I demanded.

At first, he didn't react. Then, to my surprise and chagrin, he burst out laughing.

I was taken aback. I didn't see anything funny about it. Seeing my expression of aggravation made him laugh even more. He couldn't stop. Tears rolled down his cheeks as he tried to control himself and the more he did, the more he would laugh. It was hard for me not to laugh, too. Once again laughter had relieved the tension between us.

When we both got control of ourselves, he sputtered, "That's the only reaction I get? 'What the fuck'?"

We looked at each other in amazement.

"Oh my God," I said. "We're speaking!"

I had only heard his voice on TV, except when he had whispered my name. The brogue seemed thicker, the voice deeper in person. He had never heard mine. Would he think it was melodious as some have said? I knew I spoke with an upper-class Boston accent, which I had tried to tone down. And there was a hint of a French accent. Maman and I had always spoken French together.

"So we are." He seemed at a loss. So was I.

"We've kept the silence," I said.

"Silence is God's first language."

"That may be. Now it's time to talk."

"I don't disagree."

We looked at each other.

Then we both blurted out at the same time, "Say something!"

We began to laugh.

"Wait," I said. I dropped his letter on the foot of the bed and dug the flat candles out of my purse. I lit them and turned out all of the lights except the desk lamp facing the wall. He watched me from the bed with bemusement.

"I'm sorry," he said, after quieting. "I'm afraid we're out of Jameson."

I put down the matches and walked over to the edge of the bed. I sat next to him, took his letter, and held it up to a candle.

"Wait," he said alarmed, reaching for the burning letter. "What are you doing?"

"What does it look like?" I said, pushing him away. "*Parce que c'est de la merde!*"

"Who is this chimera I have been making love to for the past week? I pour my heart out to you and you call it shit!"

He put his fingers out, making the sign of the cross.

"Would you like to go back to silence?" I asked.

"Worked for me."

"Bastard!"

The letter was almost burned down and I went to the bathroom and threw it into the toilet, flushing it away.

I came back, reached in my bag and retrieved the whiskey. I sat back on the bed, took his unicorn cup, poured him a large belt, took a sip myself and handed it to him.

"Aren't you the clever lass," he said smiling. "Where did you get it?"

"I have my suppliers," I said. "Have some."

"I think not," he said. "I have to keep my wits about me."

I took it back from him, had another sip and held it out to him again.

He didn't reach for it.

"Didn't we come here to find ourselves, Fitz?" I realized that that was the first time I had called him by his name. "Didn't we come here for metanoia, for a change of heart. Didn't we come here to find clarity and truth. Didn't we?"

"Aye," he admitted, somewhat reluctantly. I thought he seemed a little defeated.

"That letter, your letter wasn't the truth. I can't deal with this liminal space. I deserve better than that."

He didn't respond. Instead, he reached for the cup and took a large swig, then another, looking directly into my eyes for the first time since I had come into the room. There was a glimmer of a smile. An admiring smile.

"You're relentless, Ms. Sumner."

"If we had been speaking you would have realized that. If you must know the truth, I'm a honey badger. I just don't look like one."

"You fuck like one."

He reached over and gently touched my hair, smoothing it behind my ear. I felt as if I were going to lose consciousness. He took his thumb and wiped my lipstick off, then wiped it on his T-shirt. He did it again, pressing my lower lip. He leaned back against the pillows, observing my reactions, not removing his hand from my mouth. It was all I could do not to throw myself on him, but I was going to let him take the lead. He let go and looked down at my breasts encased in white cashmere. Slowly, he began to pull the zipper down, revealing glimpses of lavender lace. His casual movements only enhanced the sensuality of the moment. When he had unzipped it fully, he put one hand inside my bra and felt my breast until it was stiff. Then the other one. Before I knew it, he had my sweater off and on the floor.

He took his time with my bra, with my breasts. After he had expertly unhooked it from behind, it joined my sweater. He cupped both of my breasts in his hands, then began licking and sucking and biting them, taking turns with each.

"These are dangerous," he whispered. "A man could get hurt caught between these."

"You'll have to take your chances," I murmured.

"I'm known for my courage."

"Good thing."

"Do you think we're having too much sex?" I asked. "And not enough metanoia?"

"Sex is the path to metanoia," he assured me.

He relieved me of my yoga pants before I knew what had happened and peeled off my socks.

"How did you know I can't have an orgasm with socks on?" I asked.

"Experience. I'm an aficionado of women and socks."

"That's not all, it would seem."

His hands were on my panties, stroking the rim as he slowly inched them down, past my knees, past my ankles and to the floor.

I was now sprawled out naked on the tiny bed, lying next to him. He took his time, caressing my body with his eyes as he traced every part of it with his fingers until I thought I would expire. Still, I made no move. When I thought I couldn't stand it another minute, he reached down and pulled off his shirt, then his boxers.

"My my, Your Grace, I must say, you're in magnificent form tonight."

"Tonight?" He looked slightly dejected.

"I only said 'tonight' because I haven't been able to express my deepest admiration until now."

"I would feel remiss if I didn't offer to share my abundance with you," he teased.

I said nothing.

He brought me over on top of him and placed me just so that it would be impossible for me not to receive him. I closed my eyes and arched my back and began to undulate. He pulled me down and began kissing me, our mouths entwined as though we were drowning, desperately trying to resuscitate each other.

He began to spank me, first on one buttock and then the other. It didn't hurt, though it stung a bit. It was beyond erotic. It made me wild. I was on the verge. Then he did something that shocked me. Something that nobody had ever done to me before. He grabbed both sides of my behind and started to squeeze them, then moved one hand between and put his finger inside me. I don't even remember coming I was so overwhelmed with rapture. In the depths of my mind I heard him cry out too.

When it was over neither one of us spoke. All of this week when we couldn't talk I had longed to say something to him after we had made love.

Now it seemed unnecessary.

We were lying in each other's arms.

"I feel so happy," I said.

"Eudamonia, I think, was what Aristotle called it."

"You're a witty lover, you know."

"Lord knows I try to be inventive when I cuff. Wouldn't do to bore you."

I rolled my eyes.

"What are you thinking right now?" I asked.

"I'm not going to tell you."

"Oh yes you are. Let's play truth or dare!"

"Not on your life!"

I started to giggle. He laughed.

"Okay," I said. "You start. Ask me anything."

"What are you thinking right now?"

"I'm thinking I want to lie here forever in your arms just like this."

"That's pretty tame."

"Too tame for you?"

"Yes." He got out of the bed and walked to the door. "I want to raid the pantry. I've had nothing to eat and I'm famished."

He put on his underwear, picked mine up from the floor and began to put them on me as well.

"Let's go," he said, grabbing my hand.

"Like this?"

"It's after midnight. Everyone will be fast asleep. We just have to make it back before they go to Vigils at three-thirty. Life is full of risks, Sybilla. You only live once."

"I'll be sure to remember that."

We crept up the stairs holding hands, past Father Joseph's door, through the dining room and into the kitchen.

"What was for dinner?" he asked.

"Kielbasa and noodles, tossed salad, and applesauce. I hardly ate a bite. I was so, so . . ." I didn't finish. I didn't want to spoil our little adventure.

"Bring it on," he said. We found the leftovers in the fridge, got forks and spoons out of the white drawers and began gobbling as if we were never to see food again. When we got to the applesauce, he took his spoon and began feeding me. I did the same for him. We had applesauce running down our chins. We licked it off of each other and we kept shoveling it in, laughing and then shushing each other as we checked the door. I found some chocolate chip cookies on a baking sheet and beckoned to Fitz for us to leave. We were giggling like naughty children as we went down the stairs.

When we got back to the room, we flopped down on the bed and finished off the cookies, fighting over the last one.

"My favorite," he said, snatching it away from me.

We looked at each other and smiled.

"So," I said, stretching back on the pillows. "Spetses, huh?"

"How did you know about Spetses?" He seemed stunned.

"I did my homework, Jamie Kelly."

"I see you've found me out. My secret hiding place, my magical Greek island." He rocked onto one elbow. "But how?"

"My family owns a compound there in Palia Limani. I spend every August there. It's my magical place."

"What's your family's name."

"De Serigny."

"Jesus, Mary, and Joseph!"

We talked excitedly about Spetses, marveling at the synchronicity of it all, the fact that we both loved it, loved the same places, had the same hideaways, the time in the chapel, the pine forests, the kaikis, the tavernas. We both sighed with pleasure.

"What else do we have in common?" I asked.

"Paris," he said. "I spent two years in France working at L'Arche, a community for the intellectually challenged—"

I was stunned. Yet another coincidence. I had no idea. I didn't say anything yet.

"I know it well," I said. "It's my family's most important charity. We have supported it from the beginning. It is our passion. We have a cousin who lived at L'Arche. It's an incredible place. You asked me if I was leaving Spraig for you. In fact, I'm leaving Spraig for L'Arche. I was accepted at the Sorbonne today to be a writer in residence. I will be spending my weekends working at L'Arche."

He looked stunned. "You are going to work at L'Arche?"

"Yes. Why do you seem so surprised? I spent part of every summer volunteering there when I was growing up. I loved it even though it broke my heart. Lately, as I've been feeling so adrift, I've wondered what I was doing with my life. The writing, which has kept me alive, has not been enough. I feel called to do something more important. L'Arche was the one place I have felt drawn to."

"You will never cease to amaze me."

"How long did you stay at L'Arche?" I asked.

"Two years. Until I was called back to Dublin. I know what you mean about being heartbreaking. It was so intense. You have to be a very special person to devote your life to that kind of work. I'm not one of them. I wish I could be."

"I feel the same. But something is compelling me to go back there, to be of service rather than living a solipsistic life, always about me. Oddly, I have felt closer to the Church since I came here than I have since I was a child." I paused and looked at him. He was gazing at me in wonder.

"Did you get a break while you were there?"

"I went to Paris every weekend and stayed at Sacré-Coeur in the guest quarters. I did nothing but study French and walk the city. I know it like the back of my hand. Where does your family live?"

"Rue du Bac on the Left Bank."

"I spent a lot of my time over there. I love the Cluny Museum with the unicorn tapestries. I would go to Les Deux Magots on the Boulevard St. Germain for coffee and people-watching."

"That's where my parents met."

"Let me guess. Your favorite restaurant in Paris is L'Improviste, Gustave Eiffel's hangout."

"This is ridiculous."

"Let's think of something we don't have in common," he suggested.

"That's easy. Ireland. I've only been to Dublin once on a family trip. Tell me about Ireland. You know so much more about me and my life than I do about you."

He told me everything. About his family, his uncle Diarmid, his schooling, his band, his wild days, his decision to join the priesthood. He told me about Dierdre and we both cried in the telling. He told me about his vows to God and the penance he had undertaken. He told me about his work and his frustrations with the Church. He told me about writing his books and his fights with the Vatican. He told me he was leaving at six the next morning, that he was flying out to Rome that afternoon to have it out with them.

It was only then, when I turned away in sadness, that I saw his cassock hanging in the closet. I felt sick to my stomach. Tomorrow he would become The Archbishop of Dublin again. He would go back to his life and I to mine. Or what was left of mine. For a moment, the reality of his letter hung between us . . .

I told him about Spraig and my marriage, about his infertility and infidelity. I told him I didn't love Spraig anymore.

"What will you do?" he asked.

I looked down at my empty ring finger. "I'm going to leave him." It was first time I had said it.

He had noticed the glance to my finger. "Sybilla," he said with alarm. "I hope it's not on my account. I don't want to be the cause of your breaking up. You took vows, too."

"You may be the catalyst but you're not the cause," I assured him. "I would have eventually made this decision even if I hadn't met you."

"You're sure?"

"I applied a while ago, not really expecting to be admitted, not really thinking I would go. But when I got the email this morning I immediately said yes. I haven't told anyone about it but you. I'll be moving to Paris soon. And, I will be working at L'Arche on the weekends. I'll be living like a nun," I said with a slightly rueful smile. "I'm elated about my decision. I came here to find Sybilla. I think I may know where she has been hiding."

Fitz looked at me for a long time in wonder.

"When I first met you, even before we were speaking, I thought you were the most magical person I have ever known. You continue to amaze me with your magnificence."

He pulled me to him and held me for the longest time. "My beautiful Sybilla," he said over and over.

Both of us were in tears.

We had so little time left together. I wanted to learn more about him, everything about him.

"Tell me about your music," I said.

He paused and took me in, then said, "It's the one thing that has saved me since Dierdre died and I recommitted to God. It's a form of praying, of meditation. I lose consciousness when I'm playing, I disappear into myself. Have you seen the Whirling Dervishes? I'm in a trance. I don't know where I am. It's actually . . . it's like making love to you. Only that's even more powerful."

"Play something for me."

He got up and fetched his guitar case. He took out his instrument and fondled it lovingly, like an old friend. He pulled up his chair to the edge of the bed and started strumming. I recognized the song immediately. Another by Bono.

"You like Bono," I said. "You were playing him the other night."

"He's been my North Star until you came along."

He began playing U2's "North Star."

"Have you met him." I asked. "Bono?"

"We've shared a few pints."

"Are you composing yourself anymore?"

"Occasionally, when I'm feeling low. I miss my music . . . actually, I was trying to compose a song tonight. A song about you."

"What?"

That was unexpected.

"After I wrote that bloody letter which you so unceremoniously set ablaze, I was miserable. I thought of a song."

He fingered his guitar again and picked out a few chords as he hummed.

"I went down, down, down, to the center of my soul," he sang. "'Twas you I found, found, found, you who made me whole."

"Oh, Fitz. That's beautiful."

"You wanted the truth. That's the truth."

I got up from the bed and embraced him. He stood, picked me up in his arms, kissed me and lay me down on the bed. We were still both high, still in our underwear. Not for long.

This time our lovemaking was different. It wasn't feverish and frenzied like the other times. It was intimate, deep, and profound. It was full of beauty and serenity and grace. It was enchantment. It was beyond loving. It was soulful.

Afterward we lay in each other's arms not making a sound. We had been talking all night. The silence was welcome. He reached over and kissed my eyelids. "*Anam Cara*," he said. "My *Anam Cara*." He sat up, pulled his St. Christopher's medal over his head and placed it around my neck. "Our lovemaking is a sacrament," he said softly.

"Oh Fitz, I can't take that."

"It's the only thing I have to give you. I've never taken it off since I had my confirmation when I was thirteen. I will be with you always. I love you, Sybilla."

"*Je t'aimes aussi.*"

"*S'Aagapo*," we said in unison and laughed. It wouldn't have been real if we hadn't said it in Greek.

"Fitz?" I dreaded the answer, but I knew I had to ask. "What do you mean, it's the only thing you have to give me?" I held on to the medal, afraid he might have second thoughts.

"I mean exactly what I said. I have nothing else to give you."

"Not yourself?"

"No, Sybilla. Not myself. I can't. I'm sorry."

I felt I had been kicked in the stomach. It was such a blow. I couldn't comprehend what he was saying to me.

"Not after tonight?"

"Especially not after tonight."

I didn't say anything. I didn't know what to say. I dissolved into tears which became wracking sobs. He put his arms around me and rocked me back and forth.

"Why, Fitz? Why? I don't understand. Please help me to understand."

He was crying now too.

"God, Sybilla," he said. "I tried to explain to you in my letter. It is the most difficult decision I have ever made and the most difficult letter I have ever had to write."

"But how could you have made love to me tonight, the way we did, after you wrote that letter? What were you thinking? You're killing me. You know that. I'm dying here! You said you loved me. I believed you. You gave me your St. Christopher's medal. After you wrote that fucking letter. What kind of a person are you? And please don't tell me you are a man of God! Don't insult me like that. Or your God, for that matter. You were willing to leave your God for Dierdre and not me. What did you want from me? What do you want from me? How can you do this to me? It's cruel. It's un-Christian. You have done nothing but use me this week to assuage your own personal torment. What can I say to make you change your mind?"

"Everything you say is true, except the fact that I used you. If anything, this is more torture for me than it is for you. I will have to live with my guilt and shame for the rest of my life. I pray that it will be short. I have never been in such anguish."

"Oh please," I said. "Spare me!"

I could feel myself coming down from the high. All the joy I had felt had dissipated. Rage welled up in me and I lunged for him, beating him on his chest, punching him, slapping his face. He just took it. He didn't even try to shield himself from my blows. It was probably flagellation that he welcomed, knew he deserved. I was still crying as I was beating him. He was too. I wanted to hurt him. I wanted to kill him.

"I hate you, Fitzmaurice-Kelly," I said. "I hate you with all of my heart."

I collapsed on him and he circled his arms around me, keeping me from falling. At some point, I pulled away from him and threw myself on the bed, completely exhausted. I buried my head in my arms and lay there. He didn't move. Both of us were still naked.

There was something I needed to know. I sat up in bed.

"You've been seeing Father Joseph?"

"Aye. Several times. You?"

"Twice. He's a godsend."

"In every way . . ."

"I couldn't have made it through this week without him." I hesitated. "I told him I had met someone. That's all. I didn't say who."

He nodded his assent.

"You've told Father Joseph about us, haven't you?"

"Yes."

"What did he say?"

"He said you were beautiful inside and out. He made no judgment. He said it was a decision I had to make for myself. He couldn't or wouldn't advise me. He quoted Merton. 'We must make the choices which reveal the deepest capacities of ourselves.'"

"That wouldn't have sealed the deal. What else did he say?"

"He said that 'a life is all spiritual or not spiritual at all.' He said, 'No man can serve two masters.'"

"It was after that that you wrote the letter. You told me that you can't give me the life I deserve. You said you were committed to your vows. Well, it's not for you to decide what I deserve. That's so self-serving, so condescending. And forgive me, but you have already broken your vows this week. How can you be such a hypocrite? What's really going on here Fitz? The person standing in front of me is not the person I have fallen hopelessly in love with this week."

He took both of my hands in his, a supplicant.

"Sybilla," he said. "The truth is that I cannot resist you. I cannot stay away from you. I'm bewitched. It's as if you've cast a spell over me."

I smiled a knowing smile.

His eyes widened. "Of course you have, Sybilla," he said, emphasizing my name. "I should have guessed."

"Is it working?" I asked.

"You know it is," he said, as he released my hands. "I am not lying to you when I tell you that you are the center of my soul. You are my heart walking around outside of my body. You own me, physically, intellectually, psychologically, spiritually, in every way. Which is why I have to let you go."

"That's so cruel."

"It may seem cruel to you now, but you must trust me when I say it would be more painful for you later. What I didn't say when I was telling you about Dierdre is that I truly believe I am responsible for her death. I don't want the same thing to happen to you."

"That's just crazy."

"We believe what we believe. I believe that the deepest capacity of myself is to serve God, to do good in this world, to make a difference, to help reform the Church."

"Don't you think the best way to reform the Church is to live the book you wrote?"

"So, you read it, did you?"

"I've read everything you've written."

"As I have your work."

I took in his face. He hadn't shaved since we'd arrived and I found his stubble devastating. His eyebrows, sloping downward, gave him an irresistible look of empathy. I could barely keep myself from running my hands through his curly mop and the hair on his chest. The thing that still got me the most was his smile. Slightly inquisitive and amused, but more sad than anything.

"How could you give this up?" I asked.

"I was afraid that you would ask that. What I want for myself is you. My greatest fantasy is to leave the Church, marry you, have a family, and spend the rest of my life with you. Summers in Spetses, winters in Glendalough. Writing, making love together, caring for our children together." As he spoke, I unconsciously wrapped my hands around my stomach. "There is nothing more that I want than to be fully known and desired by you. I have thought of nothing else this week. But it is not to be. This is not about my happiness. I cannot, I will not, abjure my faith. You cannot supersede the Church but the Church cannot supersede you either. If we continued to see each other it would have to be hidden. I wouldn't be able to marry you. You would be living in the shadows, unable to love or be loved in the open. I won't be one of those priests who has hidden families outside of wedlock."

"So do you want children?"

"You're not hearing me, Sybilla. It's not about what I want. If I were with you, your life would be hell and I would be wracked with guilt.

You would learn to hate me and for good reason. I may be a hypocrite now, but I would be a much worse one if I let you be part of my life."

"How dare you decide what my life should look like?" I asked. "It's my life. I want to be with you. And I'm prepared to make sacrifices."

Fitz stood and got the blanket we'd pushed to the floor. Wrapping it around my shoulders, he said, "Of course I want children. I want to be the kind of father I never had. I can't think of anyone who would be a better mother than you. I can't think of anything more sacred than having a family with you."

"I've had my eggs frozen." I hadn't meant to say it. It just came out.

He looked at me for a long time, not speaking. I could see that he was trying to process this information, his brain in tumult over his conflicting emotions. He knew I was thirty-nine. He understood I had done that after I knew Spraig was infertile and would never allow for a sperm donor. He realized that I was saying we had time, that a decision did not have to be made instantly. There was a flicker of joy, then hope, then despair in his eyes, as I waited for his reaction.

"Sybilla," he said finally. "I am a deeply flawed person. I am a broken person. I was when I got here and I will be when I leave. Living without you is the worst punishment I could imagine except one: living with you, with your unhappiness, your disdain and contempt for me, and with our mutual guilt and shame. That I could not stand. You will see that I am right. Please tell me you understand."

"I understand," I said.

And I did. I really did. It didn't mean that my heart was not broken. Nor did it mean that I didn't wish to be dead. At that very moment, wrapped in the blanket that smelled of both of us, I wanted nothing more than to just die. But I finally did understand. I no longer hated him. In fact, in some ways I admired him for his honesty and his integrity. I knew that he was telling me the truth.

"You know that we are twin flames," I said.

"What does that mean?"

"Beings that are searching for another soul to complete them. Plato talked about souls being cut in two and yearning to find their other half. Once they are united the love between them is uncontrollable and intense. It is referred to as a 'Holy Fire.'"

"I can certainly believe that."

He smiled at me and pulled me up from the bed.

"Come dance with me," he said. "Put on some music."

The blanket still around my shoulders, I hit "Pink Martini" on Pandora.

"Shouldn't we put on some clothes?" I asked.

"Why?" Fitz murmured. "We'll just take them off again."

The music began to play. Golden Oldies. We were slow dancing. I had both arms wrapped around his neck. He had his arms around my waist. My head was buried in his neck. He began kissing mine.

"I thought we would be like Eros and Psyche. Love conquers all," I whispered.

"Sybilla, no matter what you think, the fact that we met is serendipity. It's fate. I believe it's controlled by God. We are here together now because He wanted us to be. This didn't happen without a reason. That will be revealed to us in the fullness of time."

Just then a dulcet voice began crooning a familiar sound.

"It's not for me to say you'll love me. It's not for me to say you'll always care. Oh, but here for the moment I can hold you fast. And press your lips to mine and dream that love will last."

I switched off the phone and pulled away from him, the blanket finally dropping to the floor.

"Fitz," I said. "I'm so very tired. Can we lie down?"

Without saying anything he led me to the bed and helped me into it. He went over to the desk and turned out the light. The candles had burned down long ago. He got in beside me and enveloped me in his arms.

"Did you ever read the poem 'Maud Muller'?" I asked him.

"A long time ago," he whispered. "I don't remember it. Why?"

"The last line always tears me up."

"What is it?"

"Of all the sad words of tongue or pen, the saddest are these. It might have been."

Saturday

I AWOKE LATE THE NEXT MORNING. I could see the sun pouring into the bedroom. I looked around trying to discern where I was. I felt groggy and disoriented. The room was just like mine only backward. I checked my phone. Ten a.m. It was Saturday. My plane wasn't until three so I had plenty of time to get to the airport and turn in my car. I lay back in bed, slightly chilled. The Saint Christopher's medal brushed against my breast. I looked around. There was nobody next to me. The room was empty except for my clothes which he had placed on the chair. Then I saw the closet. It was bare. His cassock was gone. He was gone. I got up and walked to the door. There on the floor was a thick ecru envelope. This time I didn't tear it open. I walked slowly to the bed, propped up the pillow and lay down.

"Angel," it said.

"The hours drag and the minutes too.

A lonesome veil brings thoughts of you.

The steepened hill—the lovely walk—
Hand in hand, heart in heart, talk and talk,
There are no words to ever say—
The joy I had that sweet soft day—
So as your heart, in its quiet beat
Reminds you that it's for me—
Know well that mine is beating for
Only always just for thee—F."

For some reason I couldn't cry. I was devoid of all feelings. I lay there staring out at the meadow. I don't know what I had expected but not this. Expected is probably not the right word. Hoped for? Prayed for? Fantasized about? He was gone. This couldn't be happening. I absolutely knew in my heart that Fitz loved me more than anything or anyone. I had zero doubt. So why did he leave? Like that? I needed to understand.

I got out of bed, threw on my clothes, and walked back to my room, leaving behind the half-empty bottle of Jameson. Let the next seeker use it to help find their way. I took a shower. I washed my hair. I brushed my teeth, I wanted to totally cleanse myself. I didn't feel dirty. I felt emotionally sullied. That clearly wasn't his intent. He was certainly in as much pain or more than I was. If only I could get inside his head, burrow into that brain, peek into the tiny crevices of his mind, maybe I could find some glimmer of comprehension.

It was time to leave. I wrote a check for my stay, more than I needed to, and put it in an envelope. I quickly packed up, threw on a white

T-shirt, jeans, and a beige blazer, and grabbed my carry-on.

As I was leaving my room I saw that the door to the chapel was open and it was empty. I felt pulled in by some kind of centrifugal force. I rolled my bag in and closed the doors, then walked up to the first row of benches and sat down, staring at the cross in front of me. This is where it all began.

I knew what I had to do. It would have to be the zenith of petitionary prayers. I had hit the nadir of my life. I absentmindedly clutched my St. Christopher's medal.

"Okay God, Jesus, Mary, and the Holy Spirit. I refuse to bargain. I refuse to threaten. I refuse to suck up. Whether I believe in you, any or all of you, is immaterial. I believe in myself, in my own power. Never mind that it took two margaritas and half a bottle of Irish whiskey to get there. Never mind that I have been in denial for most of my life. And never mind that I have been an enabler. I've enabled Spraig to abuse me, take advantage of me, diminish me during all of our relationship. He could only do that because I let him. And now Fitz. I've enabled him all of this week to seek solace in me as he has in Father Joseph. He has been using me to salve his wounds, quell his despair and his confusion. It's all been about him and his solipsistic erotic torment, which, I now suspect he actually quite enjoys. And I've played right into it. Including the sex. But the wallowing in the grief and guilt and shame. I'm beginning to get angry again. Jesus! Excuse me. He came here to find clarity. He obviously hasn't. If he had, he would be with me now. All those hours with Father Joseph! What the hell did they talk about? Him, of course. His endless suffering. I adore Father Joseph, but I must say I'm sorely disappointed in the results of his counseling. His Grace swaggers in, puts on his tight sexy black

T-shirt and jeans, pours his heart out to Father Joseph, fucks my brains out and then, without a pang, slips on his cassock and swans out of here like the archbishop he is. And leaving a pathetic, maudlin little poem behind as if to excuse himself. Bullshit!"

I don't think I had ever been in such a rage. I had come here for clarity too. I found it, then lost it, then found it, then lost it. And now . . . now I had finally found it. This time for real.

"And by the way. The four of you, God, Jesus, Mary, the Holy Spirit or whatever you are, you're not off the hook either. I've been enabling you too with my pitiful petitionary prayers. Beseeching, begging, pandering, submitting, groveling, weeping, let me count the ways. I've had it. I'm not going to play anymore. Why don't we try a little intercessory prayer? Remember what you've taught us, dear Lord. There is power in our free will and the four steps of intercession are: get informed, get inspired, get indignant, and get in sync. Well, I am there. I know everything I need to know now about Fitz and his true self. I am inspired by my own courage and power to get on with my life. And I am in sync with you all because, as I understand it, God will intervene if I get with the program. I've earned my Girl Scout badges. So, here's what I want. I want Fitz to wake up, grow up, and show up, as my old Buddhist meditation teacher taught me. She used to start every class with this Buddhist prayer. 'May all be free from sorrow and the cause of sorrow; may all never be separated from the sacred happiness which is sorrowless.' This is what I pray for Fitz. This is what I pray for myself."

The first time I came into this chapel I collapsed on the floor in tears. It was Fitz who picked me up, held me in his arms and comforted me. I half expected him to come from behind at that moment and embrace me. I listened for footsteps, but all was quiet. I was alone. As Duncan would say, it now rested with *beshert*—Yiddish for destiny.

I looked at the time. It was later than I thought. I had to get on the road. I left the chapel without glancing back, walked past the dining room and picked up an apple from the basket on the table.

As I pulled out of the driveway, I glanced wistfully over at the guest house, then up to the main chapel and the monk's quarters. It couldn't have been a more sparkling day, a brilliant recovery from the angry downpour last night. The bales of hay looked drenched but shining in the sunlight, the cows were lowing in the meadow, the birds were fluttering about and there was just the tiniest breeze fluttering the leaves. I got to the outdoor chapel, headed toward the gate and before I even knew what I was doing I veered to the left toward the river and drove down to the barn. I jumped out of the car and ran as fast as I could to the bank, to our rock, our tree.

I needed one more minute there to remember. I leaned back against the tree, listening to the gurgling of the water. In a rash moment I took off my St. Christopher's medal and lifted my arm to fling it into the Shenandoah. I couldn't bring myself to do it. It was too precious; not just to Fitz but to me. The truth was that I loved him and always would. Yes, I had been angry and hurt by his departure. But I did understand the depths of his despair, his profound anguish. He loved me. I believed with every fiber of my being that he would never do anything to deliberately hurt me. Whatever he decided, it would be what he thought was best for me, not him. I took several deep breaths, wiped my eyes, and got back on my feet.

"Goodbye," I murmured—to who or what I don't know—and turned back to the car.

I picked up my phone to check the time before I started the engine.
I had to look twice to see if I had read it right.
It was a text from him.
"Meet me on Spetses. F"

The End.

Acknowledgments

MANY YEARS AGO, Steve Case and Doug Holladay invited me to join their wonderful organization, Path North, a group focusing on how to find purpose, balance, and meaning in life. Its members are largely CEOs devoted to doing well by doing good. At the time I was invited in, I was moderating On Faith (a religion website I founded at the *Washington Post*) with Jon Meacham. Path North is well known for its many creative and imaginative events and trips. It was on a Path North excursion that I first discovered The Holy Cross Abbey in Berryville, Virginia. A group of us went for a three day silent retreat at the monastery. I had never done that before and was amazed at how meaningful it was. I went back again with Path North and then began going by myself. I found that time precious. And it was also at the monastery where I conjured up the idea of the novel. Next, I conceived of the character, James Fitzmaurice-Kelly the Archbishop of Dublin, and planned a trip to Dublin to meet and interview the real Archbishop,

Diarmid Martin. He is a fabulous person. Funny, smart, interesting, courageous, moral, and honest. Fitzmaurice-Kelly is Diarmid Martin, intellectually, morally, and spiritually.

Father James Martin is an American Jesuit priest and editor-at-large of *America Magazine*. We became friends when I was moderating On Faith. He was enormously helpful in helping me understand the role of a priest as someone who was open-minded and outspoken and brave as he is and as is Fitz Kelly.

The character of Fitz Kelly is modeled after a gorgeous Irish poet I met at Amherst College when I was at Smith College. I was a theater major and performed with the all-male cast at Amherst, which didn't admit women at the time. His name was actually Fitzmaurice Kelly and he was an older (maybe late thirties) visiting professor. He liked to hang out at rehearsals and I developed a huge, smoldering crush on him. We flirted but nothing happened and one day he just vanished, back to the Emerald Isle. I was devastated and I never saw him or heard from him again. Still, I never forgot him or his wonderful name and always fantasized about bringing him to life again, which I did in Fitz.

Father Maurice Flood, my monk counselor at Holy Cross Abbey, was a great friend of the famous American Trappist monk Thomas Merton, where they had met at the Abbey of Gethsamani in Kentucky. Father Maurice was one of the most compelling people I had ever met. We were in silence the whole time I was at the retreat. The only time one could speak was in the counseling sessions. I couldn't wait for my sessions with him. We discussed faith, philosophy, and psychology and the meaning of life in such depth that it was exhilarating. During the years when I was seeing him on my annual visits, my husband Ben Bradlee developed dementia and subsequently died. Father Maurice

ACKNOWLEDGMENTS

got me through those desolate times in a way nobody else had been able to. My gratitude toward him knows no end.

I began writing in July of 2022, which is when I met Ally Glass-Katz. Ally is a truly magical being. I hired her as a freelance editor, and sent her the few pages I had written. I had no confidence that it was any good. She wrote back immediately that it was "a masterclass" in how to open a novel. I was on my way. Writing for Ally was nothing but joy. She goaded me, prodded me, and argued with me, but mostly she cheered me on. She made me think and made me write. Her instincts were impeccable. I couldn't wait to show her the pages. Ally has worked with me all while planning a wedding, getting pregnant, and having a baby. Still, she always makes me feel as if I am her number one priority. She is a tough taskmaster. She won't take no for an answer. She works much harder than I do. She's also a kind, sympathetic, wonderful human being and she is enormously fun. We laugh all the time. I look forward to working with Ally for the rest of my life. If that isn't magic I don't know what is.

Evelyn Duffy, who had been a trusted researcher and assistant for Bob Woodward and has since started her own company, Open Boat Editing, found Ally for me and also the extraordinary researcher Minna Scherlinder Morse who can find anything, including the few lost scrolls of the Bible. Minna is relentless and will not rest until she has discovered things that don't seem discoverable.

My agent, Anne-Lise Spitzer of the Philip Spitzer Agency, took me on without hesitation and happily, she loved the novel. She worked tirelessly to sell it, consoling me through many rejections, never losing faith in the book, always on my side.

Will Wolfslau, Editorial Director at Amplify Publishing Group, is responsible for the best publishing experience I have ever had. Will got the novel immediately and was incredibly supportive. He is smart, thoughtful, and professional at every level. Lauren Magnussen, Director of Production at Amplify, has been my sherpa through the publishing process. Her follow-through is amazing. The minute I would email her I would get a response! She was beyond efficient in working with me and incredibly helpful in guiding me through the design process. Shannon Sullivan and J.C. Heins did wonderful work.

I normally hate all pictures of me but Violetta Markelou managed to take a few that I don't find horrifying. She made every effort to make me relax and not seem too posed.

Where would I be without my readers? My dear friends who took the time to read, support, console, cheer, and most importantly, advise.

Tim Shriver, one of my two spiritual advisors, was part of Path North and was on the first silent retreat we went to. After I had finished my first draft I asked him to help me with the character of Fitz Kelly. Tim is a devout Catholic and had actually considered a life in the priesthood. His advice was invaluable. He totally understood Fitz's crisis of faith and helped me understand him. Fitz would not have come alive were it not for Tim.

Jon Meacham, my other spiritual advisor, indoctrinated me into religion over a long lunch and got me started on the rather unexpected and rich path my life took, much to Ben's incredulity! I dedicated my last book *Finding Magic* to Jon. I remain forever in his debt.

Joe Hassett, one of the foremost Yeats scholars in the world, was an invaluable help to me. He went with me to Ireland, took me to Yeats's hometown of Sligo and to his grave, and tutored me in Yeats for many months. He made Fitz come alive for me.

ACKNOWLEDGMENTS

Lisa and Michael Kelley have given me the most precious gift of all. They ran a successful inn and restaurant at St. Mary's City in southern Maryland. They took our son Quinn, 8, who was dealing with learning disabilities, under their wing when we bought a farm there. They mentored him, gave him his first job at 14—first as a dishwasher, then as a server, then as a caterer—when we were told he would never be capable of doing any of those things. They showered him with love, they believed in him, and still do. My gratitude knows no bounds. And, it was Lisa who convinced me to change the ending of my book.

Leslie Marshall, a talented novelist herself, gave me support and encouragement and a perceptive analysis of the characters. She also has stood by me in the worst times of my life. She is a true friend and shares my love for Greece.

Kyle Gibson, the ultimate producer and great friend, was one of my early readers and had great advice on the evolution of Sybilla's character.

Thierry Dana, my dreamy French frère d'âme, was the most enthusiastic of all about the book. He talked it up all over the Greek island of Spetses and throughout the city of Paris. I'm going to appoint him my European publicist!

I'm grateful to Eleni and Alekos Philon, my Greek family in Spetses, who were largely responsible for my and Sybilla's affection for Spetses.

Rafe Sagalyn, legendary great agent in Washington, read the novel and was very encouraging and helpful about my publishing journey.

Richard Cohen is one my lifelong best friends and the funniest man alive. Richard, who is a twin and would have been mine if I had been one, couldn't have showered me with more praise which meant the world to me.

David Ignatius, the brilliant columnist for the *Washington Post,* is a lifelong friend as well. David is a bestselling spy novelist, so his praise for my book was seriously appreciated. He also had several valuable suggestions which I incorporated in the book. David is a kind, loyal, and thoughtful friend and a great family man.

Christiane Amanpour, a wonderful friend, extraordinarily gifted journalist, and one of the bravest people I have ever known, was an early reader and was so enthusiastic about the novel that it set me up for weeks.

Carl Bernstein and I have been through many incarnations together and have come out the other side closer than ever. Carl was immediately complimentary about the novel—a big deal from him since he is a really talented writer and reporter.

Anne Finucane is a very busy woman who took the time over and back from London to read the novel despite having to prepare for important meetings and being jet-lagged. Anne is a late-in-life friend, and we became close after Ben died and I honestly don't know how I made it this far without her in my life.

Keith Meacham, Jon's wife, my cool friend, and owner of the most exclusive shop in Nashville, read the book in Paris, the perfect place since one of the main characters is French. She had some very cogent observations.

Maureen Dowd is known as the most famous columnist in America and for good reason. Queen of Irish Americans and pretty much the journalistic Queen of Ireland, she gave me enormous help when I went to Ireland to research the book, putting me in touch with so many people that I barely had time to connect with them all. Maureen and I have been colleagues for a long, long time but since Ben died we have become closer and I value her friendship.

Peggy Dowd, Maureen's fabulous sister, really lifted my spirits when she read the novel early on and said she loved it. She also said she had been on a number of silent retreats in her life but had never had any experiences like this.

Tina Brown and I first bonded at a conference of newspaper editors at the Greenbriar resort in Virginia. She was living with the legendary British editor of the *Sunday Times*, Harry Evans, and I was living with Ben Bradlee. Both of us were much younger blondes who had run off with their editors and had caused considerable scandal. We were ostracized by the others and put in a separate wing of the hotel, much to our amusement. Tina went on to edit *Vanity Fair* and *The New Yorker* and write books, among her many accomplishments. I continued on at *The Washington Post* and wrote several books myself. Tina and Harry got married at our house in East Hampton, Grey Gardens. Later we would both have sons who had severe medical and learning problems. Harry died a few years after Ben died and we were both grieving at the same time. We don't see each other as much as I would like but I always see her as a good friend and kindred spirit.

My sister Donna, an inveterate and discriminating reader, had some good suggestions about Sybilla and her family. Donna, who lives in California, has been my life support system, a place where I can take refuge when things go badly. She is my true confidante and knows all the secrets. As Army brats, we are very close. I can't imagine what I would ever do without her.

Alexis, my nephew Christopher's wonderful wife and also an avid reader, had some thoughtful contributions about the relationship between Fitz and Sybilla.

My brother Bill Quinn, a brilliant thinker and writer, got his PhD at the University of Chicago and is a practicing Buddhist. Bill has shepherded me through some of the most difficult times in my life with his wisdom and calm. He was very helpful for me in clarifying how Sybilla dealt with her own crisis of faith and in trying to understand Fitz's.

Mary Jordan and Kevin Sullivan, friends through the years at the *Washington Post* and proud Irish Americans, introduced me to Glendalough, the magical place in Ireland where Fitz was born. I fell in love with it and fantasized about it as I do about the Shenandoah River and Holy Cross Abbey. They read the book in Ireland and were extremely supportive on their way back.

Bob Woodward and Elsa Walsh have been my rocks since Ben died, always there for me, making sure I've never been lonely. It was Watergate that brought us together. But their friendship with Ben and me and their infinite kindness has kept us together and always will. When Elsa read the book she said I had a great future in writing sex books. I took that as a compliment.

Gahl Burt's computer started reading the book out loud for her. Her daughter was in the room and asked if it was *Fifty Shades of Grey*. Gahl reads everything, mostly about foreign policy and yet was excited about the book. She lost her fabulous husband Martin Indyk this year. We all miss him terribly and I'm sad he won't be here for the book parties.

My longtime and possibly long-suffering assistant Jody Evans is my number one reader. Jody reads everything—all manner of books—and she reads everything I write. She is, as I demand, very honest. She has saved me from many mistakes and compliments me when she likes something. She also helps run my life, which is a challenge.

My best friend in college, Toni Goodale, an incredibly smart and successful business woman, took time away from her beloved Turkish TV series, which she got hooked on during Covid, to read the novel and raved. That was huge. Toni has been by my side for sixty years and always the most loyal of friends.

Olivia Nuzzi may have been my first reader and really encouraged me in her review. That meant a lot as she was the thirty-something generation I am hoping to reach.

Peter Osnos is a former *Washington Post* reporter, editor, and great friend who abandoned the *Post* to conquer the publishing world in New York, which he did, making a name for himself by signing up many of the major political and foreign policy players in the world. Peter then founded the successful publishing house Public Affairs. Peter has been my chief hand-holder through this publishing adventure, talking me off the ledge more than once. But we've made it!

Brad Graham, the owner of the fabled Politics and Prose bookstore in Washington, DC, was once a reporter at the *Washington Post,* Brad has hosted many of my former books at his book events over the years, including mine, Ben's, Katharine Grahams's, and most of my friends and colleagues. Brad was an early supporter of my publishing with Amplify. He came over for drinks one evening and made me believe I had a future in writing. He generously offered to sell my books and to have an event for me.

I asked Sandi Mendelson, the uber publicist in New York to represent me. She is really on the case and answers emails immediately and texts or emails me multiple times a day with ideas and suggestions. No issue is too small for her. My friend Susan Mecandetti, who knows the New York publishing world told me: "Everyone hates their publicists.

Everyone adores Sandi." Me too. With Sandi I'm lucky to have Melanie DeNardo and Sarah Payne working with me as well.

There are three outlets which have been invaluable to me as a writer and which I devour with regularity. Father Richard Rohr, an American Franciscan priest and writer on spirituality who runs the Center for Action and Contemplation in New Mexico writes newsletters which are always uplifting and informative. I can't get enough of Maria Popova and her blog *The Marginalian*. Nothing makes me think in so many different ways, nor enriches my mind. I find reading her exhilarating. Diana Butler Bass, among other things, publishes *The Cottage*, a spiritual blog. She is a prodigious writer and lecturer and a knowledgeable religious scholar. Reading her is always rewarding.

Robert Waldinger is a professor of psychiatry at Harvard, author of *The Good Life*, and director of the Harvard Study of Adult Development. He is also a Zen priest with whom I do group meditation sessions once a week. Bob and the sessions have changed my life in the two years since I've been participating. I find myself to be calmer, more peaceful, less agitated, and happier. This has been a Godsend since the election.

There have been some real bright spots in my life. Chris Gregorski, my physical therapist, has really brought me along after I had a stroke. His warmth, humor, sometimes sadistic exercises, determination, and friendship have made me realize that I will be doing PT forever. Mark Trudeau, my Pilates teacher, has been a gentle calming influence on me in the past year. His patience is remarkable. Chris Ulrich, the renowned Improvisor, was my teacher when I first started doing Improv two years ago and I'm still going strong, thanks to Chris. I have to say that Improv is the highlight of my week. Where else can

ACKNOWLEDGMENTS

you go and spend two-and-a-half hours with a delightful, talented group, laughing, playing, being silly, and making a fool of yourself and not being judged? It doesn't get any better than that. Especially in this toxic political environment that is Washington.

How could I not thank my hairdresser Ury Emsellem who has been cutting my hair for fifty years and seems to be able to make it look contemporary? Ury and his wife Toby and I have been through a number of tragedies and joys in our lives together and they have been a great comfort to me.

Carmen Barron has worked with me for fifteen years and runs the show here. She is a fantastic cook, a great organizer, a fixer of all things, a happy optimistic person. She is a lot of fun, but more than that she is like a mother to me. She has nursed me back to health among several surgeries and the stroke. She lives in and is always on call, no matter what time of day or night it is. I've never met anyone who worked as hard as Carmen. She is always willing to pitch in during an emergency. She is beyond loyal, loving, and caring and I never feel alone with Carmen in my life. I love her.

Yolanda Arispe, who also lives in, is a great teammate for Carmen. Yolanda has been with us for ten years and we have a lot of fun together. Yolanda works hard and takes wonderful care of me, too. And like Carmen, is never in a bad mood. She is as cheerful as Carmen which makes for a happy household. When they're not working they're out partying and dancing at night. God bless them!

Quinn, Fabiola, and Khloe are my life. Quinn and I have always been very close, as he was sick most of his life, in and out of the hospital and dealing with learning disabilities. I can't ever imagine loving anyone as much as I do Quinn. Quinn was equally close to

Ben. He adored Ben and together they bonded while working out in the woods in the country. Quinn is now forty-three and is married to the fabulous Fabiola. Fabiola's adorable twelve-year-old daughter Khloe lives with them and they have brought so much joy to our lives. It's every parent's dream to have their children live next door. Their house is attached to mine and there is a connecting door. I never go to their house uninvited but occasionally I'll look up from my desk and see Quinn absconding with a bottle of wine. Which thrills me. Quinn promised me that he would take care of me after Ben died and he did. We took care of each other until he met and fell in love with Fabiola. She has welcomed me into her wonderful family. Quinn literally saved my life when I had the stroke. They all came to the hospital and later at home to spend evenings with me so I wouldn't be alone. I will never forget their devotion and am filled with gratitude for having them in my life.

And to you, the reader—I am incredibly grateful that you're reading my book and I hope you enjoy it as much as I did while I was writing it.

About the Author

SALLY QUINN is a longtime journalist at the *Washington Post*, a bestselling novelist, and a Washington, DC insider. Her religion website "On Faith" ran in the *Washington Post* for seven years. She is the author of *We're Going to Make You a Star, Regrets Only, Happy Endings, The Party,* and *Finding Magic*. She lives and works in Georgetown.

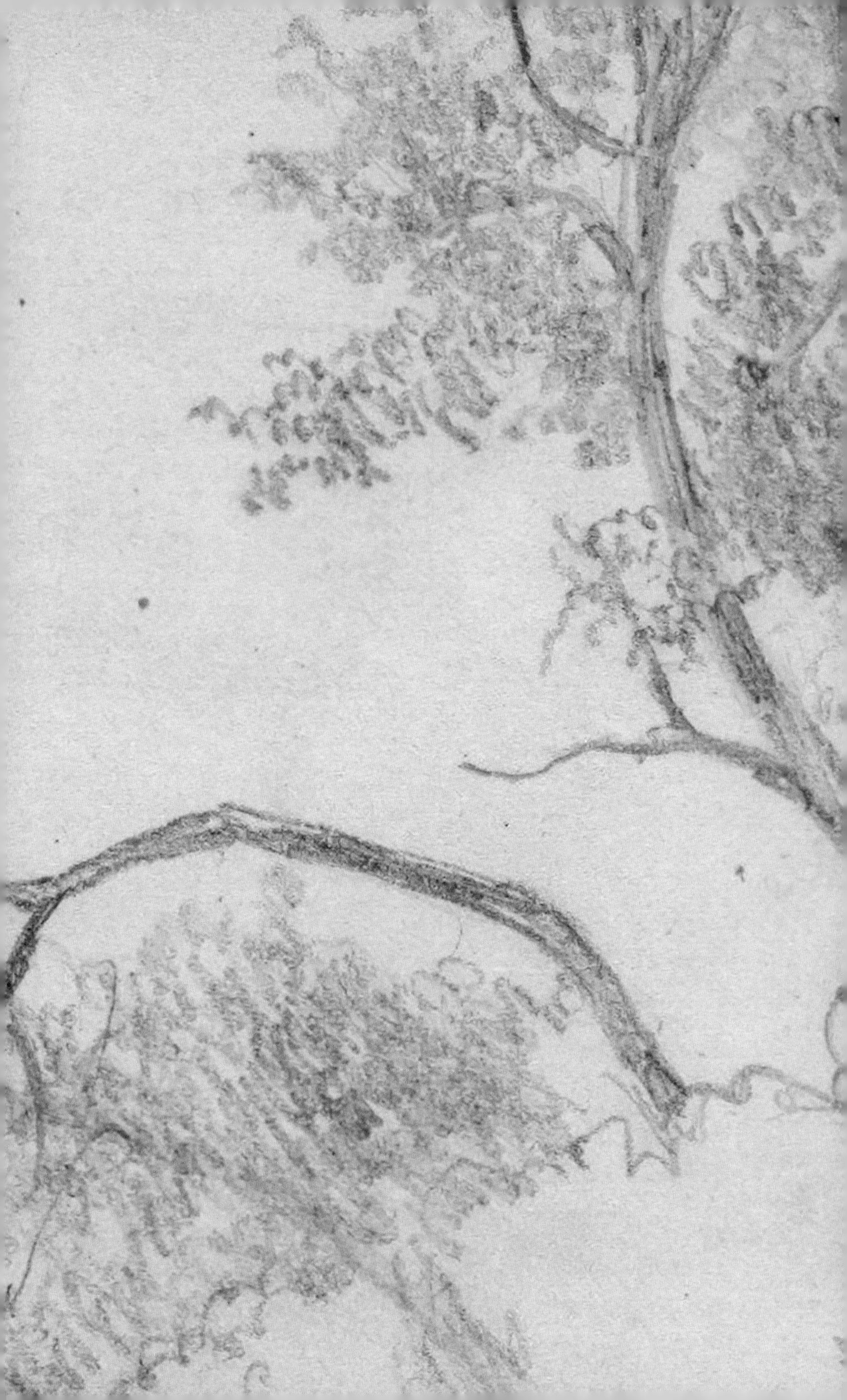

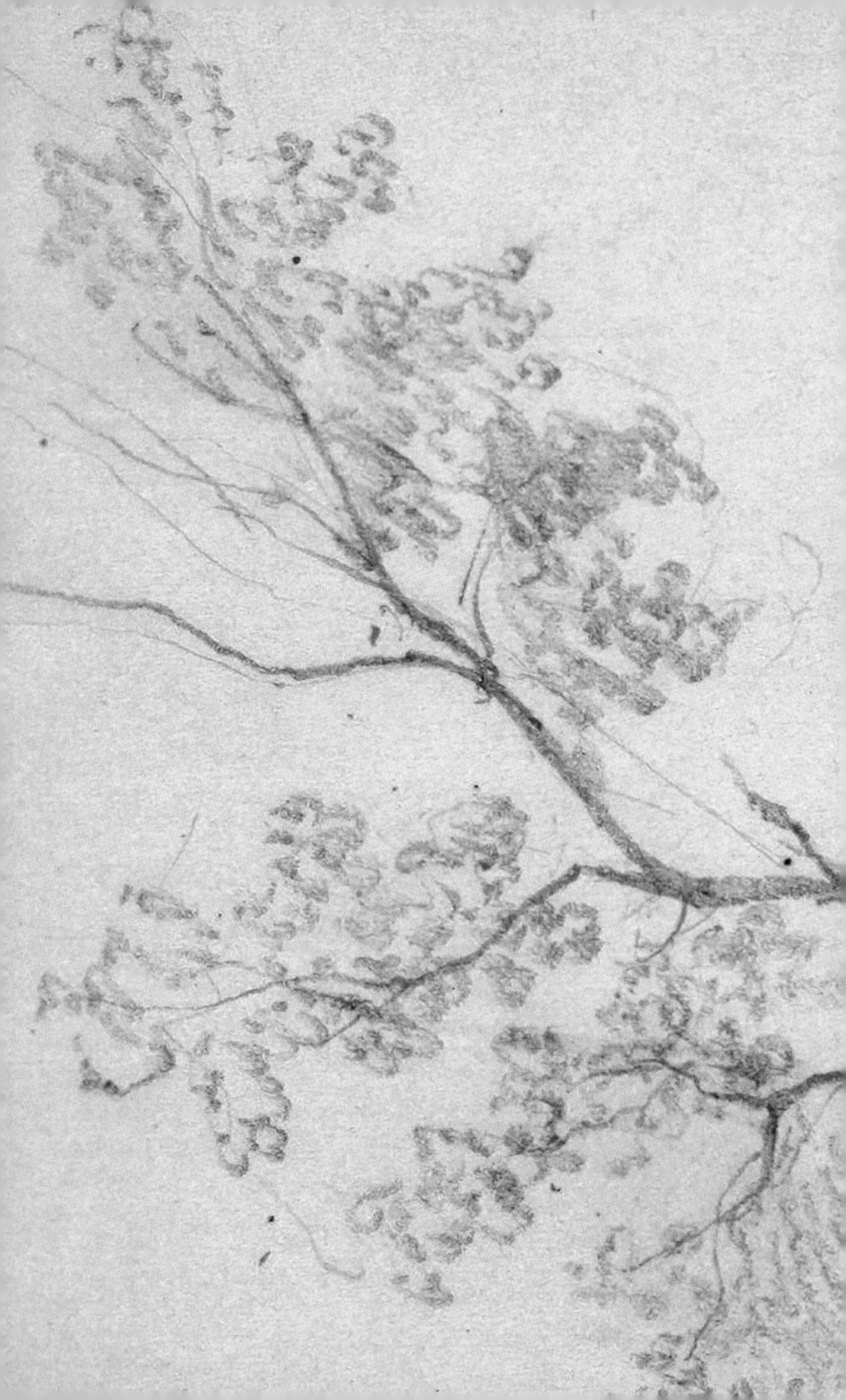